Mel Bay Presents

Mallory & McCall's Irish Pub Songbook

By
Janna McCall Geller
& Mallory Geller

For voice, guitar, mandolin, whistle and all C instruments.

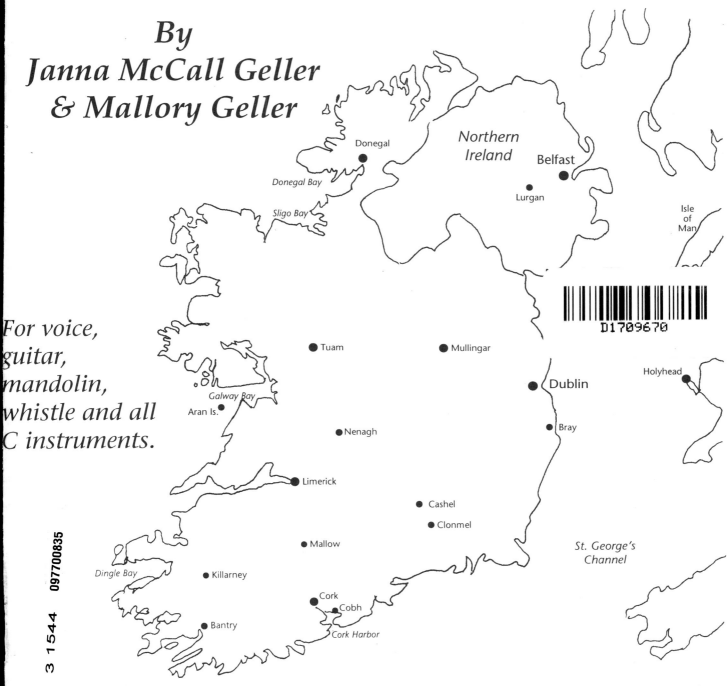

097700835

3 1544

D1709670

Visit us on the Web at http://www.melbay.com — E-mail us at email@melbay.com

Table
of Contents

Words and Music are traditional unless otherwise noted.

About the Authors

"Mallory & McCall"...

Mallory Geller and Janna McCall Geller, are collectors and performers of lively music from a variety of historic and nostalgic eras. Mallory's lusty baritone is complemented by Janna's Irish harp, vintage foot-pumped melodeon and backup vocals. They are often featured performers at Irish events, Renaissance faires, Civil War re-enactments, Victorian- and Dickensian-themed celebrations, pirate festivals, cowboy gatherings, and any number of other picturesque venues, as well as at pubs and in concert settings. Their inveterate song collecting is mirrored in their ever-growing repertoire, constantly expanding to include new fields of interest. They have been known to research and present an entirely new act for a single special event. Mallory and Janna have been married and co-creating since 1973. In addition to performing together, they have written songs, radio plays, newspaper and magazine articles, dramatic readings and more. For Mel Bay, they have collaborated on *Exploring the Folk Harp* and are finishing up a companion volume to this book titled *Mallory & McCall's Irish Ould Favorites Songbook.* They may be contacted at P.O Box 191084, Los Angeles, CA 90019.

This book is dedicated with thanks to John F. Leicester III, whose unfailing generosity of time, friendship, and love of music and musicians has graced our lives.

# *Introduction*

An Irish Pub...

The mind's eye reveals a convivial scene of comfortable good cheer, with good food and drink, good friends and good music. Most of all, music; songs and the stories they tell. For these are a tangible expression of a people's living spirit, and what this book is all about.

Here is a collection of Irish songs designed both for singing as a group or performing for a group. There are rollicking songs, sentimental songs, funny songs and even a few songs of troubles; most of all, though, these are songs to be shared, to be experienced together—in a pub, at a party or just among friends.

Many of the titles have come from the Irish folk tradition, a tradition that keeps evolving through the years, as does any musical and poetic tradition passed along from mouth to ear. They may be found in as many versions as there are singers to sing them and wordsmiths to unfold and enlarge upon the tale. So, you may find some songs you know, but not exactly as you remember them. When we've encountered multiple versions of songs, we've attempted to choose the variant that, to us, best reflects its spirit. If you don't agree, change it! Make each song your own; distill it through your own experiences and create something new, in the best folk tradition. Or, this book can be a useful reference, a consistent resource that many can share, singing and playing together.

The Irish are a race of bards—creative, spirited, ever-ready to expound upon life and living with remarkable creativity and a true love of language. The English word "whisky" is said to derive from the Irish *uisce beatha* (pronounced whiska baha)—literally the *water of life*. Throughout Irish mythos purls this living liquor, the "divil" known as poteen or mountain dew. It is claimed that the magical elixir can kill or cure, can make strong men stronger and the brave invincible, or at least can ease the spirit in times of troubles. In these songs, whisky has been given a folkloric, supernatural power that transports the imbiber far beyond mundane reality. Pure fantasy, of course, the beast becoming the beauty. But here, it is the songs that intoxicate, not the substances, themselves.

So, gather up your pots and your old tin cans, your guitars, your voices, your bones or your bodhrans and join us to share music in that Irish pub we were picturing earlier, for a metaphorical "drop of the creatur." After all, isn't music the best brew around?

Sláinte!

Mallory & McCall

PART ONE

WHISKY & RAKES, RUCTIONS & WAKES

The Hills of Connemara

The game's afoot! The distillers of illegal moonshine—"mountain tay" (tea)—had to be both keen of eye and fleet of foot if they hoped to stay one skip ahead of the government's revenue agents. The hills of Connemara are located in the west of Ireland, north of Galway Bay. "Nate" is dialectic for neat, as in drinking one's liquor straight and undiluted.

FRISKILY   Traditional

CHORUS:

CHORUS: Gather up the pots and the old tin can,
                  The mash, the corn, the barley and the bran,
                  Run like the devil from the Excise man.
                  Keep the smoke from rising, Barney!

Keep your eyes well-peeled today,
The tall, tall men are on their way,
Searching for the mountain tay
In the hills of Connemara.   *CHORUS:*

Swing to the left and swing to the right,
The Excise men will dance all night,
Drinking up the tay 'til the broad daylight
In the hills of Connemara.   *CHORUS:*

A gallon for the butcher, a quart for Dom,
A bottle for poor old Father Tom,
To help the poor old dear along
In the hills of Connemara.   *CHORUS:*

Stand your ground, it is too late;
The Excise men are at the gate!
Glory be to Paddy but they're drinking it nate
In the hills of Connemara.   *CHORUS:*

The *Moonshiner*

What sort of character keeps one eye on his still and the other peeled for the revenuers? Though there is clearly a dark side to this force—it did kill his old father—he is a fearless, footloose, independent businessman, a rugged individualist who calls 'em as he sees 'em and lets the sips fall where they may! "Wash" refers to the fermented wort from which spirits are distilled.

WITH UNDISTILLED
SATISFACTION

Traditional

I've been a moon-shin-er for man-y's the year, And I've spent all me mon-ey on whis-ky and beer. I'll go to some hol-low and I'll set up me still; And I'll make you a gal-lon for a ten shil-ling bill.

CHORUS:

I'm a ram-bler, I'm a gam-bler, I'm a long ways from home, And if you don't like me, well leave me a-lone! I'll eat when I'm hun-gry and I'll drink when I'm dry, And if moon-shine don't kill me, I'll live 'til I die.

I've been a moonshiner for many's the year,
And I've spent all me money on whisky and beer.
I'll go to some hollow and I'll set up me still;
And I'll make you a gallon for a ten shilling bill.

CHORUS: I'm a rambler, I'm a gambler, I'm a long ways from home,
And if you don't like me, well leave me alone!
I'll eat when I'm hungry and I'll drink when I'm dry,
And if moonshine don't kill me, I'll live 'til I die.

I'll go to some hollow in this country;
Ten gallons of wash—I can go on a spree.
No woman to follow, the world is all mine,
And I love none so well as I love the moonshine.   *CHORUS:*

O, moonshine, dear moonshine, O, how I love thee;
You killed me old father but dare you try me!
O, bless all moonshiners and bless all moonshine:
O, its breath smells as sweet as the dew on the vine.   *CHORUS:*

I'll have moonshine for Liza, and moonshine for Mae,
Moonshine for Lu and she'll sing all the day.
Moonshine for me breakfast, moonshine for me tay;
It's moonshine, me hearties, it's moonshine for me.   *CHORUS:*

Mountain Dew

(A Bucket of Mountain Dew)

Samuel Lover (1797-1869) was something of an Irish renaissance man whose talents included those of novelist, playwright and illustrator, in addition to songsmith. "Peelers" are a nickname for common policemen, after Sir Robert Peel, who, in 1850, instituted the Irish Constabulary. Donegal, Sligo and Leitrim are all counties in Connaught, the province that forms the west-central quarter of Ireland. "Poteen" (pronounced pwa-cheen) is home-brewed whisky, taken directly from the Irish word poitin.

BRIGHTLY

by Samuel Lover

Let gras-ses grow and wa-ters flow In a free and ea-sy way, Just give me e-nough of the fine old stuff That's made near Gal-way Bay. And Peel-ers all from Don-e-gal, Sli - go and Leit-rim, too, We'll give them the slip and we'll take a sip Of the real old moun-tain dew.

CHORUS:

High the did-dle-dee i-dol-um, Did-dle-dee doo-dle i-dol-um Did-dle-dee doo-rah did-dle-di day, High the did-dle-dee i-dol-um, Did-dle-dee doo-dle i-dol-um Did-dle-dee doo-rah did-dle-di day.

Let grasses grow and waters flow
In a free and easy way,
Just give me enough of the fine old stuff
That's made near Galway Bay.
And Peelers all from Donegal,
Sligo and Leitrim, too,
We'll give them the slip and we'll take a sip
Of the real old mountain dew.

CHORUS: High the diddle-dee idol-um,
                 Diddle-dee doodle idol-um
                 Diddle-dee doo-rah diddle-di day,
                 High the diddle-dee idol-um,
                 Diddle-dee doodle idol-um
                 Diddle-dee doo-rah diddle-di day.

At the foot of the hill there's a neat little still
Where the smoke curls up to the sky;
By the smoke and the smell, you can plainly tell
There's poteen brewing near by.
For it fills the air with perfume rare
Betwixt both me and you;
When home you roll, you can take a bowl
Or a bucket of the mountain dew.   *CHORUS:*

Now learned men as use the pen
Have wrote your praises high,
That sweet poteen from Ireland, green,
Distilled from wheat and rye.
Throw away your pills, it'll cure all ills
Be ye Pagan or Christian or Jew.
Take off your coat and grease your throat
With the real old mountain dew.   *CHORUS (twice):*

The Juice of the Barley

In County Limerick, one young fellow discovers the grand elixir and soon succumbs to its charms. It is everywhere about, and even those who rail against it must have it, after all. Limerick is in southwestern Ireland. A "gossoon" is a boy, and "turf" refers to partially carbonized layers of vegetable matter burned as a fuel. The material forms in bogs where, over time, mosses, grasses and other small plants, forming a dense, thick mat, partially decompose in water.

WITH A SWIG
AND A SWAGGER

Traditional

In the sweet Coun - ty Lim' rick one fine sum - mer's night, There were

bon - fires and fid - dlin' when I first saw the light, And the lan - ky - legg'd

mid - wife was tip - sy with joy As she danced 'round the flame with her

slip of a boy. Sing - in' *bain - ne na mó dos an gamh -*
(Sing - in' ban - ya na mo is an gan -

na, And the juice of the bar - ley for me.
na,)

In the sweet County Lim'rick one fine summer's night,
There were bonfires and fiddlin' when I first saw the light,
And the lanky-legg'd midwife was tipsy with joy
As she danced 'round the flame with her slip of a boy.

CHORUS: Singin' *bain-ne na mó dos an gamh-na,**
                 And the juice of the barley for me.

Well, when I was a gossoon of eight years or so,
With my turf and my primer to school I did go;
To a dusty old school house without any door,
Where lay the schoolmaster blind drunk on the floor.   *CHORUS:*

At the learnin' I wasn't such a genius, I'm thinkin',
But I soon bet the master entirely at drinkin'.
Not a wake or a weddin' for five miles around,
But myself in the corner was sure to be found.   *CHORUS:*

One Sunday the priest read me out from the altar,
Sayin', "You'll end up your days with your neck in a halter,
And you'll dance a fine jig between heaven and hell!"
And his words they did frighten me, the truth for to tell. *CHORUS:*

So the very next mornin' as the dawn it did break,
I went down to the vestry the pledge for to take.
And there in that room sat the priests in a bunch,
'Round a big roarin' fire drinkin' tumblers of punch.   *CHORUS:*

From that day to this I have wandered alone,
A jack of all trades, aye, and a master of none,
With the sky for my roof and the earth for my floor,
Sure, I'll dance out my days drinkin' whisky galore.   *CHORUS:*

Pronounced: banya na mo is an ganna, meaning "the milk
      of the cow for the calf."

Jug of Punch

Ah, the simple pleasures of life, this early-19th-century song tells us, all revolve around having a jug to hand. For the adventuresome, the bouncy tune lends itself to a calypso rhythm. Kerry is in the extreme southwest of Ireland. "Turf" and "peat" are often used interchangeably.

SPIRITEDLY

Traditional

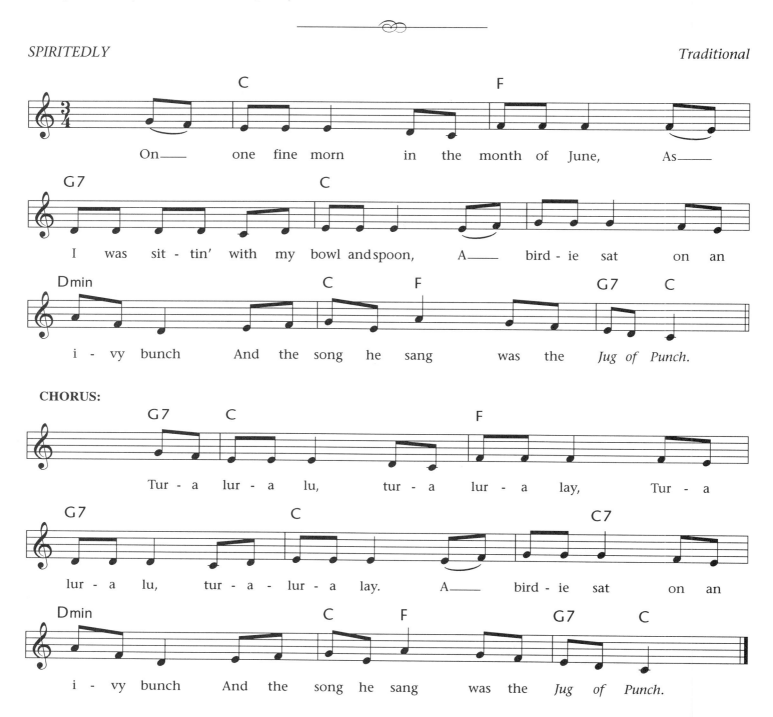

On— one fine morn in the month of June, As— I was sit - tin' with my bowl and spoon, A— bird - ie sat on an i - vy bunch And the song he sang was the *Jug of Punch.*

CHORUS:

Tur - a lur - a lu, tur - a lur - a lay, Tur - a lur - a lu, tur - a - lur - a lay. A— bird - ie sat on an i - vy bunch And the song he sang was the *Jug of Punch.*

On one fine morn in the month of June,
As I was sittin' with my bowl and spoon,
A birdie sat on an ivy bunch
And the song he sang was the *Jug of Punch*.

CHORUS: Tur-a lur-a lu, tur-a lur-a lay,
                Tur-a lur-a lu, tur-a lur-a lay.
                A birdie sat on an ivy bunch
                And the song he sang was the *Jug of Punch*.

What more diversion can a man desire
Than to court a lass by a neat turf fire,
With a Kerry pippin to crack an' crunch,
Aye, an' on the table a jug of punch.

CHORUS: Tur-a lur-a lu, tur-a lur-a lay,
                Tur-a lur-a lu, tur-a lur-a lay.
                With a Kerry pippin to crack an' crunch,
                Aye, an' on the table a jug of punch.

Learned doctors try to cure your ills
With good advise and bad-tasting pills,
But I'll let you in on my favorite hunch:
A far better cure is a jug of punch!

CHORUS: Tur-a lur-a lu, tur-a lur-a lay,
                Tur-a lur-a lu, tur-a lur-a lay.
                But I'll let you in on my favorite hunch:
                A far better cure is a jug of punch!

And when I'm dead and in my grave,
No costly tombstone will I crave;
Just lay me down in my native peat
With a jug of punch at my head and feet.

CHORUS (twice): Tur-a lur-a lu, tur-a lur-a lay,
                Tur-a lur-a lu, tur-a lur-a lay.
                Just lay me down in my native peat
                With a jug of punch at my head and feet.

A Sup of Good Whisky

This frolicsome offering suggests that, despite what people say, "all take a sup in their turn." The trick, it seems, is to sup only until mellow. The "creatur" (pronounced cray-thur) refers to whisky as a creature—something with a life of its own.

CONVIVIALLY

Words are Traditional
Music by Leo Maguire

A sup of good whis-ky will make you glad; Too much of the crea-tur will make you mad. If you take it in rea-son 'twill make you wise, If you drink to ex-cess it will close up your eyes. Yet fath-er and moth-er And sis-ter and bro-ther, They all take a sup in their turn.

A sup of good whisky will make you glad;
Too much of the creatur will make you mad.
If you take it in reason 'twill make you wise,
If you drink to excess it will close up your eyes.
Yet father and mother
And sister and brother,
They all take a sup in their turn.

Some preachers will tell you that whisky is bad;
I think so too—if there's none to be had.
Teetotalers bid you drink none at all,
But while I can get it, a fig for them all!
Both layman and brother,
In spite of this pother,
Will all take a sup in their turn.

Some doctors will tell you, 'twill hurt your health;
The justice will say, 'twill reduce your wealth.
Physicians and lawyers both do agree
When your money's all gone, they can get no fee.
Yet surgeon and doctor
And lawyer and proctor
Will all take a sup in their turn.

The Germans do say they can drink the most,
The French and Italians also do boast;
Ould Ireland's the country (for all their noise)
For generous drinking and hearty boys.
There each jovial fellow
Will drink 'til he's mellow,
And take off his glass in his turn.

The Crúiscín Lán

(Crooshkeen Lawn – The Full Little Jug)

Perhaps no other song so clearly uses the brimming little jug as a metaphor for a full and happy life, the most praiseworthy of all things. To that extent, what we have here is no less than a paean to Bacchus, and, to give the jug its due, the chorus must be sung in the original Irish!

BUOYANTLY

Traditional

Let the farmer praise his grounds, let the huntsman praise his hounds,
The shepherd praise his dewy-vested lawn.
O, but I, more blest than they, spend each happy night and day
With my darling little *crúiscín lán, lán, lán,*
O, my darling little *crúiscín lán.*

CHORUS: *Grá mo chroí mo crúiscín, sláinte geal mo mhúirnín,*
            Is grá mo chroí mo crúiscín lán, lán, lán,
            O, grá mo chroí mo crúiscín lán.

Pronounced: *Graw ma cree ma crooskeen, slawntyeh gal mavourneen,*
            Is graw ma cree ma crooshkeen lawn, lawn, lawn,
            O, graw ma cree ma crooshkeen lawn.

Meaning: My heart's love, my little jug, bright health my precious one,
            It's my heart's love, my little jug full, full, full,
            O, my heart's love, my little jug full.

Immortal and divine, great Bacchus, god of wine,
Create me by adoption thine own son;
In hopes that you'll comply, that my glass shall ne'er run dry,
Nor my smiling little *crúiscín lán, lán, lán,*
O, my smiling little *crúiscín lán.*   CHORUS:

O, when grim Death appears, in a few but happy years,
And tells me that my glass, it has run dry;
I'll say, "Begone, yeh knave! For great Bacchus gave me leave,
For to drink another *crúiscín lán, lán, lán,*
O, to drink another *crúiscín lán!*"   CHORUS:

Then fill your glasses high, let's not part with lips so dry,
Though the lark now proclaims it is the dawn;
And since we can't remain, may we shortly meet again,
To fill another *crúiscín lán, lán, lán,*
O, to fill another *crúiscín lán.*   CHORUS:

All For Me Grog

A warning against overindulgence? Hardly! The singer's up-tempo energy proves his remorsefulness for past sins of excess is actually nothing more than lip service. "Grog" can be any spiritous liquor, but most often refers to rum diluted with water.

ALE AND HEARTY   *Traditional*

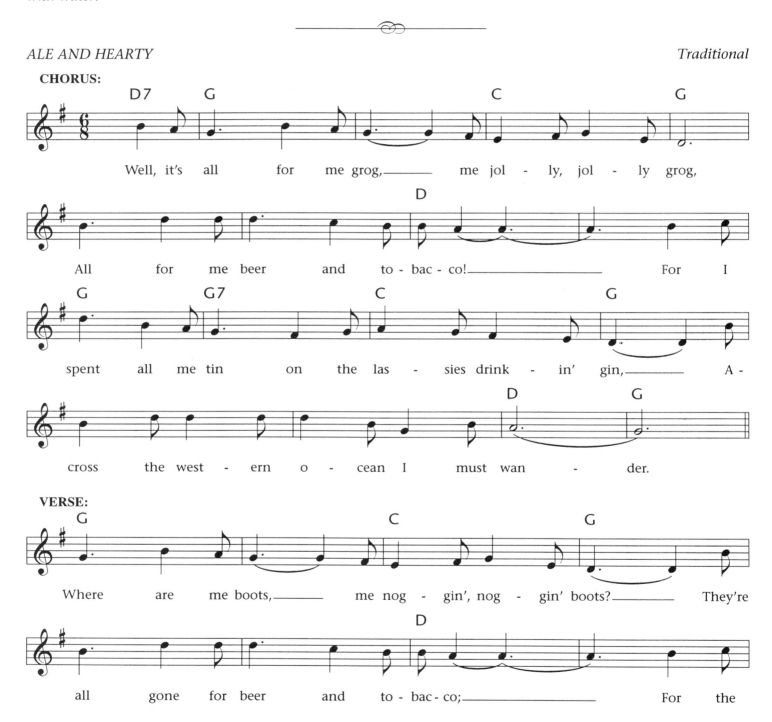

CHORUS:

Well, it's all for me grog, me jol - ly, jol - ly grog,

All for me beer and to - bac - co! For I

spent all me tin on the las - sies drink - in' gin, A -

cross the west - ern o - cean I must wan - der.

VERSE:

Where are me boots, me nog - gin', nog - gin' boots? They're

all gone for beer and to - bac - co; For the

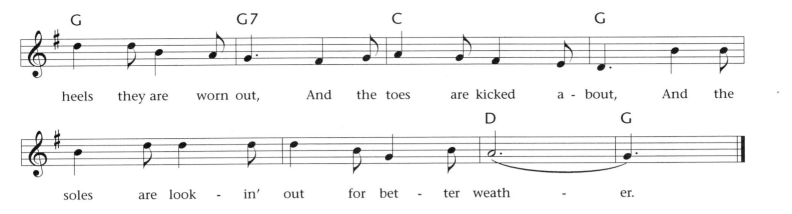

heels   they are   worn out,   And   the   toes   are kicked   a - bout,   And   the

soles   are   look - in'   out   for   bet - ter   weath -   er.

CHORUS: Well, it's all for me grog, me jolly, jolly grog,
All for me beer and tobacco!
For I spent all me tin on the lassies drinkin' gin,
Across the western ocean I must wander.

Where are me boots, me noggin', noggin' boots?
They're all gone for beer and tobacco;
For the heels they are worn out,
And the toes are kicked about,
And the soles are lookin' out for better weather.   *CHORUS:*

Where is me shirt, me noggin', noggin' shirt?
It's all gone for beer and tobacco;
For the collar is all worn,
And the sleeves, they are all torn,
And the tail is lookin' out for better weather.   *CHORUS:*

I'm sick in the head and I haven't been to bed
Since first I came ashore from me slumber;
For I spent all me dough
On the lassies, don't you know.
Far across the western ocean I must wander.   *CHORUS (twice!):*

Dicey Riley

Though Dicey Riley is clearly unable to get along without frequent sips of the elixir of life, she remains "the heart of the rowl"—the salt of the earth—as far as her Dublin intimates are concerned.

LIVELY

Traditional

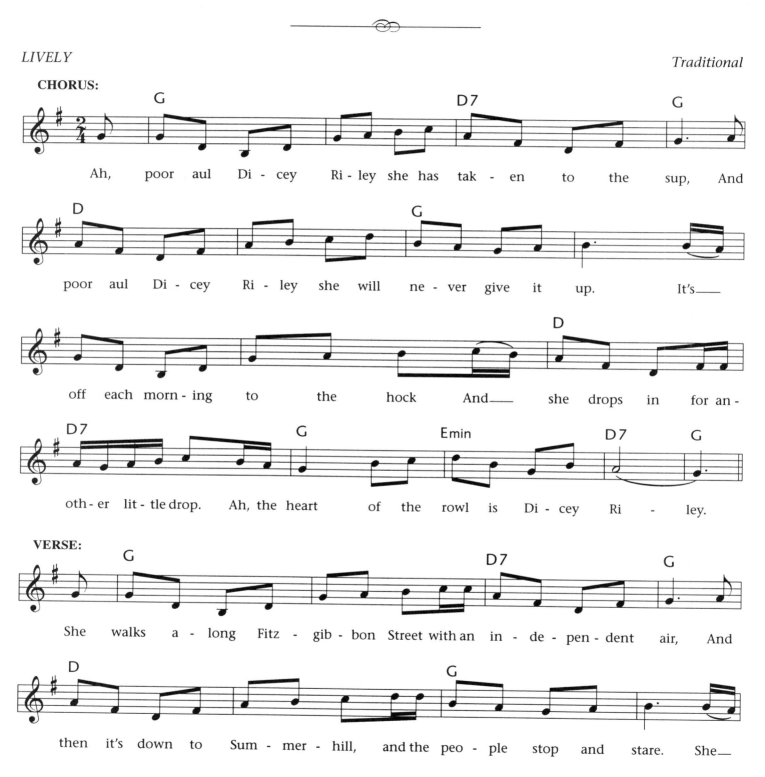

CHORUS:

Ah, poor aul Di - cey Ri - ley she has tak - en to the sup, And poor aul Di - cey Ri - ley she will ne - ver give it up. It's off each morn - ing to the hock And she drops in for an - oth - er lit - tle drop. Ah, the heart of the rowl is Di - cey Ri - ley.

VERSE:

She walks a - long Fitz - gib - bon Street with an in - de - pen - dent air, And then it's down to Sum - mer - hill, and the peo - ple stop and stare. She

says, "It's near-ly half-past one, And it's time I had an-

oth-er lit-tle one." Ah, the heart of the rowl is Di-cey Ri-ley.

CHORUS: Ah, poor aul Dicey Riley she has taken to the sup,
And poor aul Dicey Riley she will never give it up.
It's off each morning to the hock
And she drops in for another little drop.
Ah, the heart of the rowl is Dicey Riley.

She walks along Fitzgibbon Street with an independent air,
And then it's down to Summerhill, and the people stop and stare.
She says, "It's nearly half-past one,
And it's time I had another little one."
Ah, the heart of the rowl is Dicey Riley.   CHORUS:

She owns a little sweetshop at the corner of the street,
And every evening after school I go to wash her feet.
She leaves me there to mind the shop
While she nips in for another little drop.
Ah, the heart of the rowl is Dicey Riley.   CHORUS:

Three Drunken Ladies

These three Ladies are a pubowner's dream—or nightmare! Take your pick. The Isle of Wight is an island county in the south of England. Its mild climate and varied scenery have made it a frequent resort destination.

WITH AN ABUNDANCE
OF SAUCE

Words adapted by Mallory Geller
Air: Three Drunken Maidens

There were three drunk-en La - dies came down from the Isle of Wight; They

start-ed to drink on Mon - day, nev-er stopped 'til Sat - ur - day night. Well,

Sat-ur-day night it came, me lads, but still they wouldn't get out; No,

these three drunk-en La - dies, they pushed the jug a - bout. Yes!

These three drunk-en La - dies, they pushed the jug a - bout.

There were three drunken Ladies came down from the Isle of Wight;
They started to drink on Monday, never stopped 'til Saturday night.
Well, Saturday night it came, me lads, but still they wouldn't get out;
No, these three drunken Ladies, they pushed the jug about.
Yes! These three drunken Ladies, they pushed the jug about.

Then in came dancing Sally, her cheeks a rosy bloom.
"Shove o'er, you jolly sisters, and give young Sal some room;
And I will be your equal before this evening's out!"
But they'd brook no competition as they pushed the jug about.
Yes! These three drunken Ladies, they pushed the jug about.

They had woodcock and pheasant, partridge and hare,
And of every sort of dainty, no shortage was there there,
They'd thirty gallons and more, me lads, but still they wouldn't get out;
No, these three drunken Ladies, they pushed the jug about.
Yes! These three drunken Ladies, they pushed the jug about.

Then in came the landlord, and to them had this to say:
"Thirty pounds for drink, me girls, is what you'll have to pay!"
They had drunk ten pounds a-piece, me lads, but still they wouldn't get out;
No, these three drunken Ladies, they pushed the jug about.
Yes! These three drunken Ladies, they pushed the jug about.

Where are your fancy hats and your mantles rich and fine?
They've all been swallowed up, me girls, as tankards of fine wine.
And where are your fancy men, young Ladies frisk and gay?
They've left you in the ale house and it's there you'll have to stay.
Yes! These three drunken Ladies, they pushed the jug about.

Now, many years have passed, me lads, yet even to this day,
The three sit at that table having drunk their lives away.
Yes, so much did they take, me lads, they're preserved like pickl'd trout,
As though they might before your eyes still push the jug about.
Yes! These three drunken Ladies, they pushed the jug about.

Nancy Whisky

Originally of Scottish origin, here is an example of loving the living liquid not too wisely, but too well!

WITH WRY
SOBRIETY

Traditional
Music adapted by Mallory & McCall

I am a weav-er, a Cal-ton weav-er, I am a rash and a rov-in' blade. I've got sil-ver in my brit-ches, And I fol-low the rov-in' trade.

CHORUS: Whis-ky, whis-ky, Nan-cy Whis-ky, Whis-ky, whis-ky, Nan-cy, O!— Whis-ky, whis-ky, Nan-cy Whis-ky, Whis-ky, whis-ky, Nan-cy, O!—

I am a weaver, a Calton weaver,
I am a rash and a rovin' blade.
I've got silver in my britches,
And I follow the rovin' trade.

CHORUS (twice):   Whisky, whisky, Nancy Whisky,
                           Whisky, whisky, Nancy, O!

As I went down through Glasgow City,
Nancy Whisky I chanced to smell.
I went in, sat down beside her;
Seven long years I loved her well.   *CHORUS:*

The more I kissed her, the more I loved her;
The more I kissed her, the more she smiled.
Soon I forgot my mother's teachin',
Nancy Whisky had me beguiled.   *CHORUS:*

"Come on, landlady, what's the reck'nin'?
Tell me what I have to pay."
"Fifteen shillin's is the reck'nin';
Pay me quickly and go away!"   *CHORUS:*

Well, I rose early in the mornin'—
To slake my thirst, it was my need.
I tried to rise but I was not able;
For, Nancy had me by the knees.   *CHORUS:*

Now, I'm goin' back to the Calton weavin';
I'll surely make them shuttles fly.
Aye, I'll make far more at the Calton weavin'
Than ever I did in my rovin' way.   *CHORUS:*

So, come all you weavers, you Calton weavers;
Come all you weavers, where e'er you be.
Beware of whisky, Nancy Whisky;
She'll ruin you like she ruined me.   *CHORUS:*

Garryowen

The lads from Garryowen ought to be spanked for their behavior, but they do it to a great tune. Garryowen is in County Limerick. "Spa" is mineral water.

ROWDILY

Attributed to Dan L. Howell

Let— Bac - chus' sons— be not— dis - mayed, But—

join— with me— each jo - vi-al blade; Come— booze— and sing,— and

lend— your aid To help— me with— the cho - rus:

CHORUS:

In - stead of Spa we'll drink brown ale, And— pay the reck - 'ning on the nail; No

man for debt shall go— to jail From Gar - ry - o - wen in glo - ry!

Let Bacchus' sons be not dismayed,
But join with me each jovial blade;
Come booze and sing, and lend your aid
To help me with the chorus:

CHORUS: Instead of Spa we'll drink brown ale,
                  And pay the reck'ning on the nail;
                  No man for debt shall go to jail
                  From Garryowen in glory!

We are the boys that take delight in
Smashing the Lim'rick lamps when lighting,
Thro' the streets like sporters fighting
And tearing all before us.   *CHORUS:*

We'll break windows, we'll break doors,
The watch knock down by threes and fours;
Then let the doctors work their cures
And tinker up our bruises.   *CHORUS:*

We'll beat the bailiffs out of fun,
We'll make the mayor and sheriffs run,
We are the boys no man dares dun
If he regards a whole skin.   *CHORUS:*

Our hearts, so stout, have got us fame,
For soon 'tis known from whence we came;
Where'er we go they dread the name
Of Garryowen in glory.   *CHORUS:*

Johnny Connell's tall and straight,
And in his limbs he is complete;
He'll pitch a bar of any weight
From Garryowen to Thomond Gate.   *CHORUS:*

Garryowen is gone to wrack
Since Johnny Connell went to Cork,
Though Darby O'Brien leaped over the dock
In spite of all the soldiers.   *CHORUS:*

The Rakes of Mallow

Having encountered the lads from Garryowen, one wonders if anyone else's youthful exuberance could possibly do more damage. Now meet the cocks-of-the-walk from Mallow, a town in County Cork, in the south of Ireland. Since County Cork and County Limerick share a common border, perhaps these two groups of rogues competed head-on for the championship of hell-raising. It looks to us like a toss-up, right down to the doing of their misdeeds to a fast, catchy air. This is one of the many Irish classics used by Victor Young in his score for the film, The Quiet Man.

ROWDILY – 2

Traditional
Air is The Galway Piper

Beau - ing, belle - ing, danc - ing, drink - ing,— Break - ing win - dows,

swear - ing, sink - ing,— Ev - er rak - ing, nev - er think - ing,

Live— the— Rakes— of— Mal - low. Spend - ing— fas - ter

than it comes, Beat - ing— wait - ers, bai - liffs, duns, Bac - chus'— true be -

got - ten sons, Live— the— Rakes— of— Mal - low.

Beauing, belleing, dancing, drinking,
Breaking windows, swearing, sinking,
Ever raking, never thinking,
Live the Rakes of Mallow.
Spending faster than it comes,
Beating waiters, bailiffs, duns,
Bacchus' true begotten sons,
Live the Rakes of Mallow.

One time nought but claret drinking,
Then like politicians, thinking,
Raising funds when funds are sinking,
Live the Rakes of Mallow.
Living short but merry lives,
Going where the Devil drives,
Having sweethearts, but no wives,
Live the Rakes of Mallow.

Racking tenants, stewards teasing,
Swiftly spending, slowly raising,
Wishing thus to spend their days in
Raking, as at Mallow.
Then, to end this raking life,
They get sober, take a wife.
Ever after live in strife.
Wishing e'er for Mallow.

Monto

Monto was the locals' nickname for Montgomery Street, a notorious red-light and party district near the Dublin Customhouse, closed down in 1925. This tune is chock full of meaning, now obscured by age, but we've found it great fun guessing at the references. Here are a few that are still familiar: a "mot" is woman, a girlfriend or a date; a "bowler" is a derby hat; a "growler" is a Clarence, a closed, four-wheel carriage; "childer" is dialectic for children; "Vicky" refers to Queen Victoria; the "Phoenix" is Phoenix Park, one of Europe's largest, located just northwest of the center of Dublin; the "Garda" is the Home Guard or police; "stone" is a measure of weight equal to 14 pounds; and "póg mo thóin" (pronounced pogue mahone) is Irish for "kiss my backside."

RUDELY   by George Hodnett

Well, if you've got a wing-o, take her up to ring-o,
Where the waxies sing-o all the day.
If you've had your fill of porter and you can't go any further,
Then give your man the order: "Back to the Quay!"
      And take her up to Monto, Monto, Monto.
      Take her up to Monto. Langeroo ! ! to you.

You've heard of the Duke of Gloucester, the dirty old imposter,
He got a mot and lost her up the furry glen.
He first put on his bowler, then he buttoned up his trousers
And he whistled for a growler, and he says, "My man:
      Take me up to Monto, Monto, Monto.
      Take me up to Monto." Langeroo ! ! to you.

You've heard of the Dublin Fusiliers, the dirty old bamboozileers,
They went and got the childer, one, two, three.
Oh, marching from the Linen Hall, there's one for every cannon ball
And Vicky's going to send them all o'er the sea.
      But first go up to Monto, Monto, Monto.
      But first go up to Monto. Langeroo ! ! to you.

When Carey told on Skin-the-goat, O'Donnell caught him on the boat,
He wished he'd never been afloat, the filthy skite!
It wasn't very sensible to tell on the Invincibles;
They stood up for their principles, day and night.
      And they all went up to Monto, Monto, Monto.
      And they all went up to Monto. Langeroo ! ! to you.

Now, when the Czar of Russia and the King of Prussia
Landed in the Phoenix in a big balloon,
They asked the Garda band to play *The Wearing of the Green*,
But the buggers in the depot didn't know the tune!
      So they both went up to Monto, Monto, Monto.
      So they both went up to Monto. Langeroo ! ! to you.

Now, the Queen, she came to call on us, she wanted to see all of us;
I'm glad she didn't fall on us, she's eighteen stone!
"Mr. Neill, Lord Mayor, " says she, "is this all you've got to show me?"
"Why, no, ma'am, there's some more to see: *póg mo thóin!*"
      And he took her up to Monto, Monto, Monto.
      And he took her up to Monto. Langeroo ! ! to you.
      Let's all go up to Monto, Monto, Monto.
      Let's all go up to Monto. Langeroo ! ! to you.

The Waxies Dargle

The Waxies Dargle was the annual outing of the Dublin candlemakers to Bray, a seaside town in County Wicklow, on Ireland's east coast, south of Dublin. This traditional tune is also used for The Girl I Left Behind Me, *popular both in Ireland and in the American west (see* The Songs of Ireland *by Jerry Silverman, published by Mel Bay Publications).* A "boozer" is a pub or other place for drinking, and "braces" are men's suspenders.

BRIGHTLY   Traditional

Says— my aul' wan to your aul' wan: Will yeh come to the Wax - ies

Dar - gle? Says— your aul' wan to my aul' wan: Sure, I have - n't got a

far - thin'. I've just been down to Mon - to Town To see Un - cle Mc -

Ar - dle, But he would - n't lend me half a crown To go to the Wax - ies

CHORUS: Dar - gle. What are yeh hav - in', will yeh have a pint? Yes, I'll

have a pint with you, sir, And if one of you does - n't

or - der soon We'll be thrown out of the booz - er.

Says my aul' wan to your aul' wan:
Will yeh come to the Waxies Dargle?
Says your aul' wan to my aul' wan:
Sure, I haven't got a farthin'.
I've just been down to Monto Town
To see Uncle McArdle,
But he wouldn't lend me half a crown
To go to the Waxies Dargle.

CHORUS: What are yeh havin', will yeh have a pint?
                  Yes, I'll have a pint with you, sir,
                  And if one of you doesn't order soon
                  We'll be thrown out of the boozer.

Says my aul' wan to your aul' wan:
Will yeh come to the Galway races?
Says your aul' wan to my aul' wan:
With the price of me aul' lad's braces.
I went down to Capel Street
To the cheapskate money lender,
But he wouldn't give me a couple of bob on
Me aul' lad's red suspenders.   *CHORUS:*

Says my aul' wan to your aul' wan:
We have no beef or mutton
But if we go down to Monto Town
We might get a drink for nuttin'.
Here's a piece of good advice
I got from an aul' fishmonger:
When food is scarce and yeh see the hearse
Yeh'll know yeh have died of hunger.   *CHORUS:*

The Holy Ground

The Holy Ground was another red-light district, this one near the docks of the Cobh *(pronounced cove) of County Cork in the south of Ireland. As the ships slipped their moorings, the sailors bid their "ladies" goodbye by shouting, "Fine girl you are!"*

SPORTINGLY   *Traditional*

Fare thee well to you my Di - nah, A thous - and times a - dieu. We are say - ing good - bye to the Ho - ly Ground and the girls we all love true. We will sail the salt seas o - ver And then re - turn to shore. And still I live in hope to see The Ho - ly Ground once more.

Fare thee well to you my Dinah,
A thousand times adieu.
We're saying goodbye to the Holy Ground
And the girls we all love true.
We will sail the salt seas over
And then return to shore.
And still I live in hope to see
The Holy Ground once more.

CHORUS: (shout) *Fine girl you are!*
            You're the girl I do adore.
            And still I live in the hope to see
            The Holy Ground once more.
            (shout) *Fine girl you are!*

And now the storm is rising,
I see it coming soon,
For the night is dark and dreary,
You can scarcely see the moon.
And the good old ship, she is tossing about,
The riggin' is all tore.
And still I live in hope to see
The Holy Ground once more.   *CHORUS:*

At last the storm is over
And we are safe on shore,
We will go into a public house
To the girls who we adore.
And we'll drink strong ale and porter
And we'll make the rafters roar,
And when our money is all spent
We'll go to sea for more.   *CHORUS:*

Whisky, You're the Devil

If whisky is the devil, here it just might be the imp of courage—the courage a young man would need to take his best girl and flee his native soil rather than be impressed into an army bound to fight another country's battles far from home. "March" is a country's border, and a "firelock" is another name for a flintlock rifle.

BRISK MARCH

Traditional

O, now, brave boys, we'll run for march, Not off to Por-tu-gal and Spain. The drums are beat-ing, the ban-ners fly-ing, The dev-il a home will find to-night.

CHORUS:

Love, fare thee well, With me tith-ree-i the doo-dle-i the dum, With me tith-ree-i the doo-dle-i the dum, Me rikes-fol toor-a-lad-die O, there's whis-ky in the jar. *Hey!* Whis-ky, you're the dev-il, You're lead-ing me a-stray, O-ver hills and moun-tains and to A-mer-i-

cay.   You're   sweet - er,   strong - er,   de - cent - er,   You're   spunk - i - er   than

tay.   O,——   whis - ky,   you're   me dar - ling,   drunk   or   so - ber.

O, now, brave boys, we'll run for march,
Not off to Portugal and Spain.
The drums are beating, the banners flying,
The devil a home will find tonight.

CHORUS: Love, fare thee well,
             With me tith-ree-i the doodle-i the dum,
             With me tith-ree-i the doodle-i the dum,
             Me rikes-fol toor-a-laddie
             O, there's whisky in the jar. Hey!

             Whisky, you're the devil,
             You're leading me a-stray,
             Over hills and mountains and to Americay.
             You're sweeter, stronger, decenter,
             You're spunkier than tay.
             O, whisky, you're me darling, drunk or sober.

O, the French are fighting boldly,
Men are dying hot and coldly;
Give every man his flask of powder,
His firelock on his shoulder.   CHORUS:

Says the mother, "Do not wrong me,
Don't take me daughter from me,
For if you do I will torment you,
And after me death me ghost will haunt you!"   CHORUS:

The Wild Rover

This pub song is very popular, perhaps because even if one can't sing, one can always clap! "Custom" is another word for patronage.

RAMBUNCTIOUSLY

Traditional

I've been a wild ro - ver for ma - ny's the year, And I spent all my mon - ey on whis - ky and beer. But now I'm re - turn - ing with gold in great store, And I nev - er will play the wild ro - ver no more.

CHORUS:

And it's no! nay! nev - er! No, nay, ne - ver, no more Will I play the wild ro - ver, No, ne - ver, no more!

I've been a wild rover for many's the year,
And I spent all my money on whisky and beer.
But now I'm returning with gold in great store,
And I never will play the wild rover no more.

CHORUS: And it's no! nay! never! *[clap, clap, clap, clap!]*
No, nay, never no more
Will I play the wild rover,
No, never, no more!

I went to an ale house I used to frequent,
And I told the landlady my money was spent.
I asked her for credit; she answered me, "Nay,
Such a custom like yours I could have any day!"   *CHORUS:*

Then I took from my britches ten sovereigns bright,
And the landlady's eyes opened wide with delight.
Said she, "I have whisky and wines of the best—
And the words that I spoke, sure, were only in jest."   *CHORUS:*

I'll go home to my parents, confess what I've done,
And I'll ask them to pardon their prodigal son.
And if they caress me, as oft times before,
Sure, I never will play the wild rover no more!   *CHORUS (twice!):*

Bould Thady Quill

(The Muskerry Sportsman)

This melody is a variant of Nell Flaherty's Drake, *printed elsewhere in this volume, but with a rousing chorus that begs for group participation. Imagine the jubilant sportsmen (and maids!) gathered to celebrate the triumph of their own darlin' hero with a pint and a boisterous song. Banteer is in County Cork about 10 miles west of Mallow, while Killarney is a bit further west over the border in County Kerry. Hurling, a sport similar to field hockey, has been called the national pastime of Ireland. "Bate" is dialectic for beat, and "colleen," meaning a girl, is taken directly from the Irish* cailín.

Words by Mr. Gleeson of West Cork, 1905
Air is a variant of Nell Flaherty's Drake

WITH SPIRITS

CHORUS:

For ramb-lin', for rov-in', for foot-ball or court-in', For
drink-in' black por-ter as fast as you'd fill, In all your days rov-in' you'll
find none so jo-vial As our Mus-ker-ry sports-man, the Bould Tha-dy Quill.

O, ye maids of Dunhollow, who're anxious for courtin',
A word of advice I will give unto ye:
Proceed to Banteer, to the athletic sportin',
And hand in your names to the club committee.
And never commence any sketch in your program
'Til a carriage you see flyin' over the hill,
Right down thro' the valleys and glens of Kilcorney
With our own darlin' sportsman, the Bould Thady Quill.

> *CHORUS:*   For ramblin', for rovin', for football or courtin',
> For drinkin' black porter as fast as you'd fill,
> In all your days rovin' you'll find none so jovial
> As our Muskerry sportsman, the Bould Thady Quill.

The great hurlin' match between Cork and Tipperary
'Twas played in a park on the banks of the Lee,
And our own darlin' lads were afraid of bein' beaten,
So they sent for Bold Thady, to Balinagree.
He hurled that ball right and left in their faces,
And showed them Tipperary men action and skill.
If they touched on his lines, he would certainly brain them,
And the papers were full of the praise of Thad Quill.   *CHORUS:*

Here's a health to the sportsmen of Ireland, so merry,
Whose hearts are as stout and as brave as can be,
What bate all the hurlers from Galway to Kerry
With their captain, Bould Thady from Ballinagree.
For whether it's fightin' or courtin' or blarney,
For teasin' and squeezin' our lad "tops the bill";
Sure, all the fair colleens from here to Killarney
Are daft and crazy on Bould Thady Quill.   *CHORUS:*

At the Cork exhibition there was a fair lady
Whose fortune exceeded a million or more,
But a bad constitution had ruined her completely
And medical treatment had failed o'er and o'er.
"Arragh, mother," says she, "sure I know what will ease me
And cure this disease which will certainly kill.
Give over your doctors and medical treatments;
I'd rather one squeeze out of Bould Thady Quill!"   *CHORUS:*

❀ Sylvest ❀

(Big Strong Man)

These rhythmic lyrics and big beat suggest that the Irish may have invented rap music. Well... maybe not. This pub favorite mentions the 1910 James Jeffries-Jack Johnson world heavyweight title fight, the 1915 sinking of the Lusitania and 1919 champion Jack Dempsey. Later versions use the names of later champions. Our hero living in a "caravan" may indicate that he's a traveler, an Irish gypsy.

WITH A BIG,
STRONG BEAT

Traditional

Have you heard a-bout the big, strong man? He lives in a car-a-van. Have you heard a-bout the Jef-fries-John-son fight? Oh, what a hell of a fight! You can take all the hea-vy-weights you got,_____ We got a lad who can beat the whole lot. He used to ring the bells in the bel-fry; Now he's gon-na fight Jack Demp-sey.

CHORUS:

(Shout!)

Was me broth-er,___ Syl-vest. *What's he got?* A row of for-ty med-als on his chest. *Big Chest!* He killed fif-ty bad men in the West; He knows no

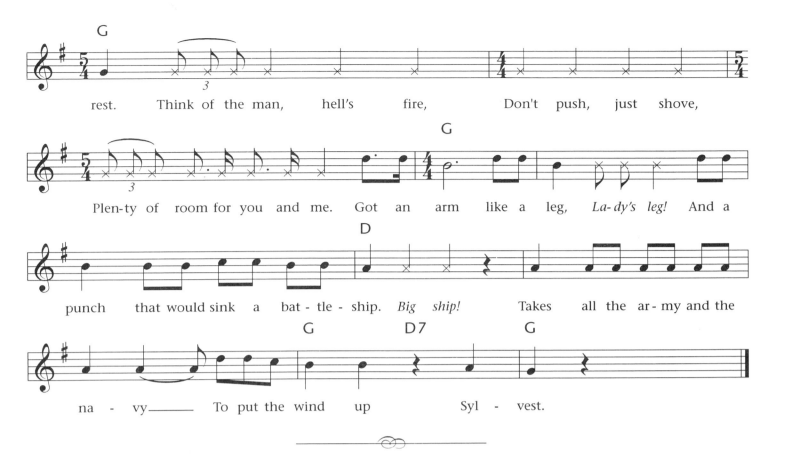

Have you heard about the big, strong man?
He lives in a caravan.
Have you heard about the Jeffries-Johnson fight?
Oh, what a hell of a fight!
You can take all the heavyweights you got,
We got a lad who can beat the whole lot.
He used to ring the bells in the belfry;
Now he's gonna fight Jack Dempsey.

CHORUS:
> Was me brother, Sylvest.
> *(Spoken) What's he got?*
> A row of forty medals on his chest.
> *(Spoken) Big chest!*
> He killed fifty bad men in the West;
> He knows no rest.
> *(Spoken) Think of the man, hell's fire,*
> > Don't push, just shove,
> > Plenty of room for you and me.
> Got an arm like a leg,
> *(Spoken) Lady's leg!*
> And a punch that would sink a battleship.
> *(Spoken) Big ship!*
> Takes all the army and the navy
> To put the wind up Sylvest.
> > [Last time: *(Spoken) Big Deal!*]

He thought he'd take a trip to Italy,
He thought that he'd go by sea.
He dove off the harbor in New York
And he swam like a madman for Cork.
He saw the Lusitania in distress—
(Spoken) What'd he do?
He put the Lusitania on his chest.
(Spoken) Big chest!
Drank all the water in the sea,
And he walked all the way to Italy.   *CHORUS:*

He thought he'd take a trip to old Japan,
So they brought out the big brass band.
He played every instrument they'd got,
What a lad, he played the whole lot!
The old church bell will ring,
The old church choir will sing.
They all turned out to say farewell
To me big brother, Sylvest.

                                          CHORUS:

The Galway Races

Think of the excitement—so many sights and sounds and smells to encounter traveling from the countryside into the city to take part in one of the year's biggest events! People truly are assembling from "all quarters of the nation": Nenagh is in County Tipperary, Aran is a group of three islands in Galway Bay and County Clare lies just to their south, while Dublin is on the east coast and Cork is on the south coast. A "crubeen" is a pig's foot. "Thimbles and Garters" are games of chance. The "Fenians" were a secret society whose aim was the overthrow of British Rule in Ireland. "Fáilte" (pronounced fail-tyeh) is Irish for welcome. And a fine time being had by all!

AT A GALLOP   Traditional

As I rode down to Gal - way Town to seek for re - cre - a - tion On the

sev - en - teenth of Au - gust, me mind b'ing el - e - vat - ed, There were

mul - ti - tudes as - sem - bled with their tick - ets at the sta - tion._____ Me

eyes be - gan to daz - zle and I'm going to see the rac - es. With me

whack fol - de - da fol - de dith - er - y id - le day._____

As I rode down to Galway Town to seek for recreation
On the seventeenth of August, me mind b'ing elevated,
There were multitudes assembled with their tickets at the station.
Me eyes began to dazzle and I'm going to see the races.
With me whack fol-de-da fol-de dith-er-y id-le day.

There were passengers from Limerick and passengers from Nenagh,
And passengers from Dublin and sportsmen from Tipp'rary;
There were passengers from Kerry and all the quarters of the nation,
And our member, Mr Hasset, for to join the Galway Blazers.
With me whack fol-de-da fol-de dith-er-y id-le day.

There were multitudes from Aran and members from New Quay Shore,
The boys from Connemara and the Clare unmarried maidens,
There were people from Cork City who were loyal, true and faithful,
That brought home the Fenian prisoners from dying in foreign nations.
With me whack fol-de-da fol-de dith-er-y id-le day.

It's there you'll see confectioners with sugarsticks and dainties,
The lozenges and oranges, the lemonade and raisins,
The gingerbread and spices to accommodate the ladies
And a big crubeen for thruppence to be picking while you're able.
With me whack fol-de-da fol-de dith-er-y id-le day.

It's there you'll see the gamblers, the thimbles and the garters,
And the sporting Wheel of Fortune with the four and twenty quarters.
There were others without scruple pelting wattles at poor Maggie,
And her father well-contented and he looking at his daughter.
With me whack fol-de-da fol-de dith-er-y id-le day.

It's there you'll see the pipers and the fiddlers competing,
And the nimble-footed dancers and they tripping on the daisies.
There were others crying, "Cigars and lights and bills of all the races,
With the colours of the jockeys and the prize and horses' ages."
With me whack fol-de-da fol-de dith-er-y id-le day.

It's there you'll see the jockeys and them mounted on most stately,
The pink and blue, the orange and green, the emblem of our nation.
When the bell was rung for starting all the horses seemed impatient,
I thought they never stood on ground their speed was so amazing.
With me whack fol-de-da fol-de dith-er-y id-le day.

There was half a million people there of all denominations,
The Catholic, the Protestant, the Jew and Presbyterian.
There was yet no animosity no matter what persuasion
But *fáilte* and hospitality inducing fresh acquaintance.
With me whack fol-de-da fol-de dith-er-y id-le day.

The Rocky Road to Dublin

Here is a whole different look at coming from the country to the city, in this case all the way across Ireland from Tuam, a town in the Connaught country of the west, to Dublin, with a stop at Mullingar, about half-way between. Holyhead is directly across the Irish Sea on the coast of Wales. If you've mastered The Galway Races, a real rocky road is successfully singing this song in tempo—it's considered a sort of performer's rite of passage. A "blackthorn" is a cane or stick made from this hard, spiny wood. The word "brogue" has two meanings. First, referring to shoes, usually of stout coarse leather. Second, referring to an Irish accent, it is taken from the Irish word, barróg, meaning a wrestling grip, the idea being that if someone's pronunciation is different from one's own, it must be the result of his being, literally, tongue-tied. "Paddy" is a nickname for Patrick and, by extension, for any Irishman, sometimes used pejoratively. "Rig" is probably short for rigadoon, a lively dance, and a "shillelagh" is a cudgel made of an oak or blackthorn sapling.

FAST

Traditional
Words from a 19th-century broadsheet
Air is taken from a slip-jig

In the mer-ry month of May from my home I start-ed, Left the girls of Tuam, near-ly bro-ken heart-ed; Sa-lu-ted fa-ther dear, kissed me dar-lin' mo-ther, Drank a pint of beer, me grief and tears to smo-ther. Then, off to reap the corn and leave where I was born, I cut a stout black-thorn to ban-ish ghost and gob-lin; In a bran' new pair of brogues, I rat-tled o'er the bogs, And fright-ened all the dogs on the rock-y road to Dub-lin.

CHORUS:

One, two, three, four, five. Hunt the hare and turn her down The rock-y road and all the way to Dub-lin. Whack fol-ol de-da.____

In the merry month of May from my home I started,
Left the girls of Tuam, nearly broken-hearted;
Saluted father dear, kissed me darlin' mother,
Drank a pint of beer, me grief and tears to smother.
Then, off to reap the corn and leave where I was born,
I cut a stout blackthorn to banish ghost and goblin;
In a bran' new pair of brogues, I rattled o'er the bogs,
And frightened all the dogs on the rocky road to Dublin.

CHORUS: One, two, three, four, five. Hunt the hare and turn her down
The rocky road and all the way to Dublin. Whack fol-ol de-da.

In Mullingar that night I rested limbs so weary;
Started by daylight next morning light and airy.
Took a drop of the pure, to keep me heart from sinkin',
That's the Paddy's cure, whene'er he's on for drinkin',
To see the lassies smile, laughin' all the while
At me curious style, 'twould set your heart-a-bubblin';
They ax'd if I was hired, the wages I required,
'Til I was almost tired of the rocky road to Dublin.   *CHORUS:*

In Dublin next arrived, I thought it such a pity
To be so soon deprived a view of that fine city.
When I took a stroll all among the quality,
Me bundle it was stole all in that neat locality.
Somethin' crossed my mind, then I looked behind,
No bundle I could find on me stick a-wobblin';
Enquirin' for the rogue, they said me Connaught brogue
Wasn't much in vogue on the rocky road to Dublin.   *CHORUS:*

From there I got away, me spirits never failin',
Landed on the Quay as the ship was sailin'.
Captain at me roared, said that no room had he
When I jumped aboard, a cabin found for Paddy
Down among the pigs, I played some funny rigs,
Danced some hearty jigs, the water 'round me bubblin'.
When off Holyhead I wished meself was dead
Or better far, instead, on the rocky road to Dublin.   *CHORUS:*

The boys of Liverpool, when we safely landed,
Called meself the fool, I could no longer stand it;
Blood began to boil, temper I was losin',
Poor old Erin's Isle they began abusin'.
"Hurrah, me soul!" said I, me shillelagh I let fly,
Some Galway boys came by, they saw I was a-hobblin';
With a loud hurray, they joined in the affray
And quickly cleared the way for the rocky road to Dublin.   *CHORUS:*

—————— 49 ——————

Rattlin' Bog

There are as many versions of this song as you can add on items to the verse. Once you've got The Galway Races *and* The Rocky Road to Dublin *well in hand, an interesting variation is to try to sing each* Rattlin' *verse, no matter how long, in one breath! Mallory has made it one of his showpieces.*

AT YOUR OWN RISK!   *Traditional*

CHORUS:

O, roe, the rat-tlin' Bog, the Bog down in the Val-ley-O,

O, roe, the rat-tlin' Bog, the Bog down in the Val-ley-O.

VERSE ONE:

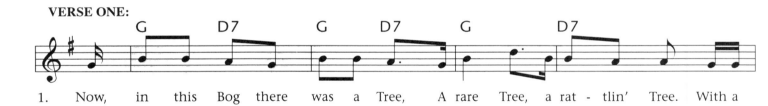

1. Now, in this Bog there was a Tree, A rare Tree, a rat-tlin' Tree. With a

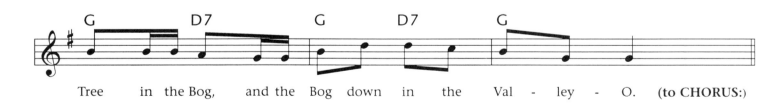

Tree in the Bog, and the Bog down in the Val-ley-O. **(to CHORUS:)**

VERSE TWO THROUGH...?

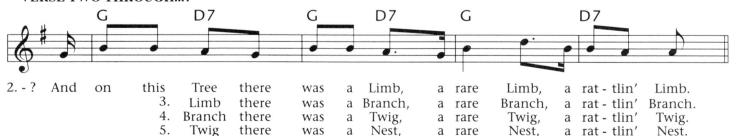

2.-? And on this Tree there was a Limb, a rare Limb, a rat-tlin' Limb.
3. Limb there was a Branch, a rare Branch, a rat-tlin' Branch.
4. Branch there was a Twig, a rare Twig, a rat-tlin' Twig.
5. Twig there was a Nest, a rare Nest, a rat-tlin' Nest.

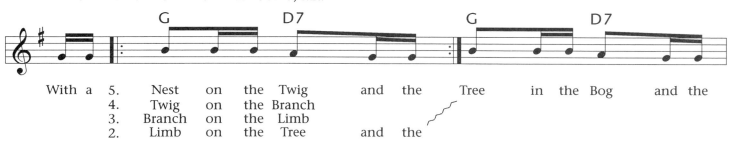

With a
5.   Nest   on   the   Twig   and   the   Tree   in the   Bog   and the
4.   Twig   on   the   Branch
3.   Branch on   the   Limb
2.   Limb   on   the   Tree   and   the

ADD ON AS MANY ITEMS AS YOU LIKE!

Bog   down   in   the   Val - ley - O.

CHORUS: O, roe, the rattlin' Bog, the Bog down in the Valley-O,
                 O, roe, the rattlin' Bog, the Bog down in the Valley-O.

1. Now, in this Bog there was a Tree,
   A rare Tree, a rattlin' Tree.
   With a Tree in the Bog,
   And the Bog down in the Valley-O.   *CHORUS:*

2. And on this Tree there was a Limb,
   A rare Limb, a rattlin' Limb.
   With a Limb on the Tree,
   And the Tree in the Bog,
   And the Bog down in the Valley-O.   *CHORUS:*

3. And on this Limb there was a Branch,
   A rare Branch, a rattlin' Branch.
   With a Branch on the Limb,
   And the Limb on the Tree,
   And the Tree in the Bog,
   And the Bog down in the Valley-O.   *CHORUS:*

4. And on this Branch there was a Twig...

5. And on this Twig there was a Nest...

6. And in this Nest there was an Egg...

7. And on this Egg there sat a Bird...

8. And on this Bird there was a Wing...

9. And on this Wing there was a Feather...

10. And on this Feather there was a Barb...

11. And on this Barb there was a Flea...

12. And on this Flea there was a Hair...

13. And on this Hair there was a Mite...

14. And on this Mite there was a Germ...

Mite,	Wing,	Branch,
Hair,	Bird,	Limb,
Flea,	Egg,	Tree,
Barb,	Nest,	Bog,
Feather,	Twig,	Valley-O!

Paddy Lay Back

In the give and take of this rollicking, swollicking chantey, the swabbies echo the last words of each line.

Traditional

WITH A
YO HEAVE HO

It was a cold and drear - y morn - ing in Dec-em - ber, (Dec - em - ber) And
all of me mon-ey be - ing spent, (be - ing spent) What day it was I
hard - ly can re-mem - ber, (re - mem - ber) When down to the ship-ping of-fice I
went. (there I went) That day there was a great de-mand for
sail - ors (sail - ors) From the Col - o- nies, from Fris - co and from
France. (and from France) So, I shipped on board the lin - er called the Hots-pur
(Hots - pur) And got par-a-lyt - ic drunk on me ad - vance. (me ad - vance)

CHORUS:

Oh, Pad-dy lay back, (Pad-dy lay back) Take in your stack, (take in your

52

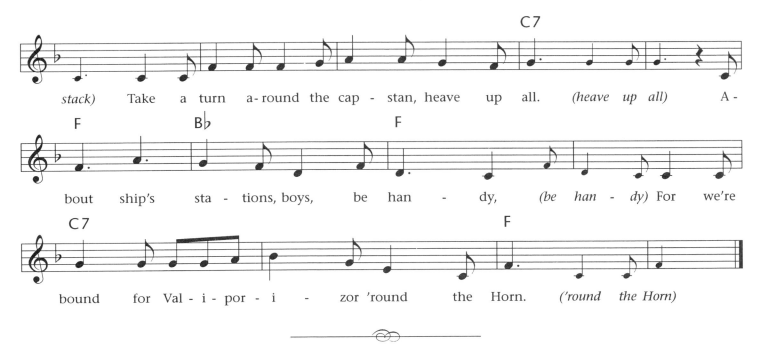

stack) Take a turn a-round the cap - stan, heave up all. *(heave up all)* A-

bout ship's sta - tions, boys, be han - dy, *(be han - dy)* For we're

bound for Val - i - por - i - zor 'round the Horn. *('round the Horn)*

It was a cold and dreary morning in December, *(December)*
And all of me money being spent, *(being spent)*
What day it was I hardly can remember, *(remember)*
When down to the shipping office I went. *(there I went)*

That day there was a great demand for sailors *(sailors)*
From the Colonies, from Frisco and from France. *(and from France)*
So, I shipped on board the liner called the Hotspur *(Hotspur)*
And got paralytic drunk on me advance. *(me advance)*.

CHORUS: Oh, Paddy lay back, *(Paddy lay back)*
             Take in your stack, *(take in your stack)*
             Take a turn around the capstan, heave up all. *(heave up all)*
             About ship's stations, boys, be handy, *(be handy)*
             For we're bound for Valiporizor 'round the Horn. *('round the Horn)*

Now, some of our fellows had been drinking, *(been drinking)*
And me, meself, was heavy on the booze, *(on the booze)*
So I sat upon me old sea chest a-thinking *(a-thinking)*
I'll just turn in and have meself a snooze. *(have a snooze)*

Well, I wished I was in the Jolly Sailors *(Sailors)*
Along with Irish Paddies drinking beer, *(drinking beer)*
Then I thought what a jolly lot are sailors *(sailors)*
And with me flipper I wiped away a tear. *(wiped a tear)*   CHORUS:

Well, we got all the tugs up along side, *(along side)*
They towed us from the wharf and out to sea, *(out to sea)*
With half the crew just hanging o'er the ship's side *(the ship's side)*
And the bloody row that started sickened me. *(sickened me)*

Well, the bosun, he said he couldn't savvy us, *(savvy us)*
The crews were speaking lingos all galore, *(all galore)*
So the only thing the old man could do was *(could do was)*
Pay us ugly sailors off and ship some more. *(ship some more)*   CHORUS:

The Mermaid

Superstitious sailing men considered the sighting of a mermaid to be the worst kind of bad luck. There are versions of this 19th-century tune sung throughout the English-speaking world. Bantry is in County Cork, in Ireland's extreme southwest.

LIVELY –
FOR NOW--_-_!

Traditional

'Twas Fri - day morn when we set sail, And we were not far from the land, When our Cap - tain, he spied a mer - maid so fair With a comb and a glass in her hand.

CHORUS:

And the o - cean waves do roll, And the storm - y winds do blow; And we poor sail - ors go skip - ping to the top, While the land - lub - bers lie down be - low, be - low, be - low, While the land - lub - bers lie down be - low.

'Twas Friday morn when we set sail,
And we were not far from the land,
When our Captain, he spied a mermaid so fair
With a comb and a glass in her hand.

CHORUS: And the ocean waves do roll,
                And the stormy winds do blow;
                And we poor sailors go skipping to the top,
                While the landlubbers lie down below, below, below,
                While the landlubbers lie down below.

Then up spake the Captain of our gallant ship,
And a fine old man was he:
"The fishy mermaid has warned me of our doom;
We shall sink to the bottom of the sea!"   *CHORUS:*

Then up spake the mate of our gallant ship,
And a well-spoken man was he:
"I have me a wife in Bantry by the sea
And tonight a widow she will be."   *CHORUS:*

Then up spake the cabin-boy of our gallant ship,
And a brave young lad was he:
"There's nary a soul in Bantry by the sea
Who shall shed a single tear for me."   *CHORUS:*

Then up spake the cook of our gallant ship,
And a crazy old butcher was he:
"I care much more for my kettles and my pans
Than I do for the bottom of the sea."   *CHORUS:*

Then three times 'round spun our gallant ship,
And three times 'round spun she;
Then three times 'round spun our gallant ship
And she sank to the bottom of the sea.   *CHORUS:*

The
Irish Rover

Sailors are famous for telling tall tales and so are the Irish. So, when you have an Irish sailor telling you the story of his ship, crew and cargo, it becomes a whale of a tale, indeed! "Bet" is dialectic for beat. The River Lee runs east from the Cork highlands down to Cork Harbor, while the Bann runs northwest from the Mourne Mountains in County Down through County Armagh and then north into the Atlantic Ocean. County Tyrone is also in the north, while County Westmeath is in central Ireland, west of Dublin, and Dover is in southern England.

BRIGHT
AND BLUSTERY

Traditional

In the year of our Lord eigh-teen hun - dred and six We set sail from the coal quay of Cork. We were sail - ing a - way with a car - go of bricks For a grand cit - y hall in New York. We'd an el - e - gant craft, She was rigged fore and aft, And how the trade winds drove_____ her; She had twen - ty - three masts and she stood sev - 'ral blasts, And they called her the Ir - ish Ro - ver.

In the year of our Lord eighteen hundred and six
We set sail from the coal quay of Cork.
We were sailing away with a cargo of bricks
For a grand city hall in New York.
We'd an elegant craft,
She was rigged fore and aft,
And how the trade winds drove her;
She had twenty-three masts and she stood sev'ral blasts,
And they called her the Irish Rover.

There was ould Mickey Coote who played hard on his flute
When the ladies lined up for a "set,"
He would tootle with skill for each sparkling quadrille
'Til the dancers were fluthered and bet.
With his smart witty talk he was "cock o' the walk,"
As he rowl'd the dames under and over.
When he took up his stance they all knew at a glance
That he sailed on the Irish Rover.

There was Barney Magee from the banks of the Lee,
There was Hogan from County Tyrone,
There was Johnny McGurk who was scared stiff of work,
And a chap from Westmeath named Malone.
There was Slugger O'Toole,
Who was drunk as a rule,
And fighting Bill Tracy from Dover;
And your man Mick McCann from the banks of the Bann,
Was the skipper on the Irish Rover.

We had one million bags of the best Sligo rags,
We had two million barrels of bone;
We had three million bales of old nanny goat's tails,
We had four million barrels of stone.
We had five million hogs
And six million dogs,
And seven million barrels of porter;
We had eight million sides of old blind horses' hides
In the hold of the Irish Rover.

We had sailed seven years when the measles broke out
And our ship lost her way in a fog;
And the whole of the crew was reduced down to two:
'Twas myself and the captain's old dog.
Then the ship struck a rock,
O Lord, what a shock,
And nearly tumbled over;
Turned nine times around, then the poor old dog was drowned.
I'm the last of the Irish Rover.

Rosin the Bow (Beau)

Some tunes are fortunate enough to lead many lives. In America, for example, the supporters of Abraham Lincoln's 1860 presidential campaign knew it as Lincoln and Liberty, *the abolitionist movement penned* The Liberty Ball *to its rolling cadences, and there is a folk song from the Pacific Northwest,* Acres of Clams, *all sharing the tune of this Irish original. A "hogshead" is a large cask or barrel.*

SPRYLY   Traditional

I've trav-ell'd this world all o-ver And now to an-oth-er I go, Where I know that good quar-ters are wait-ing For to wel-come old Ros-in the Bow.

CHORUS:

To wel-come old Ros-in the Bow, (me lads,) To wel-come old Ros-in the Bow, And I know that good quar-ters are wait-ing For to wel-come old Ros-in the Bow.

I've travell'd this world all over
And now to another I go,
Where I know that good quarters are waiting
For to welcome old Rosin the Bow.

CHORUS: To welcome old Rosin the Bow, (me lads,)
To welcome old Rosin the Bow,
And I know that good quarters are waiting
For to welcome old Rosin the Bow.

When I'm dead and laid out on the counter,
A voice you will hear from below,
Saying, "Send down a hogshead of whisky,
We'll drink to old Rosin the Bow."

CHORUS: We'll drink to old Rosin the Bow, We'll drink... etc

Now, get a half-dozen stout fellows
And stack them all up in a row;
Let them drink out of half-gallon bottles
To the mem'ry of Rosin the Bow.

CHORUS: To the mem'ry of Rosin the Bow, etc...

Then take this half-dozen stout fellows
And make them all stagger and go
And dig a great hole in the meadow
And in it put Rosin the Bow.

CHORUS: And in it put Rosin the Bow, etc...

Get ye a couple of bottles,
Put one at me head and me toe;
With a diamond ring scratch out upon them
The name of old Rosin the Bow.

CHORUS: The name of old Rosin the Bow, etc...

I feel that old tyrant approaching,
That cruel remorseless old foe,
And I lift up me glass in his honor—
Take a drink with old Rosin the Bow!

CHORUS: Take a drink with old Rosin the Bow, (me lad,) etc...

Look at the Coffin

(Isn't It Grand, Boys?)

The Irish are well-known for their wakes, for giving the deceased a jolly send-off, or at least the friends and family a memorable party. Here and following are two different takes on Irish wakes.

WITH MOCK
SOBRIETY

Traditional

Look at the cof - fin_____ with its gold - en han -

dles;_____ Is - n't it grand, boys,_____ to be blood - y well

CHORUS:

dead? Blood - y well dead! Let's not have a snif - fle,_____ Let's

all have a blood - y good cry,_____ And al - ways re - mem - ber the

long - er you live, The soon - er you'll blood - y well die._____

Look at the coffin with its golden handles;
Isn't it grand, boys, to be bloody well dead?
Bloody well dead!

CHORUS: Let's not have a sniffle,
                 Let's all have a bloody good cry,
                 And always remember the longer you live,
                 The sooner you'll bloody well die.

Look at the flowers, all bloody withered.
Isn't it grand, boys, to be bloody well dead?
Bloody well dead!   CHORUS:

Look at the mourners, bloody great hypocrites!
Isn't it grand, boys, to be bloody well dead?
Bloody well dead!   CHORUS:

Look at the preacher, bloody sanctimonious!
Isn't it grand, boys, to be bloody well dead?
Bloody well dead!   CHORUS:

Look at the widow, bloody great keener!
Isn't it grand, boys, to be bloody well dead?
Bloody well dead!   CHORUS:

*Look at the whisky, bloody great whisky!
 Isn't it grand, boys, to be bloody well dead?
 Bloody well dead!

FINAL CHORUS: Let's not have a snifter,
                        Let's all have a bloody hogshead!
                        And always remember the more that you drink
                        The better you'll feel when you're dead!

* This last is our variant of a verse sung by Marooned, an a capella chantey crew
  shipwrecked in Las Vegas.

Tim Finnegan's Wake

In this famous song, whisky meets its ultimate challenge, and prevails! Performers have a choice of doing this tune either in tempo, or freely as a recitative. A "hod" refers to bricks, mortar, concrete and the like carried by laborers to supply bricklayers. "Mavourneen" means my darling. A "gob" is a mouth, a "row" is a fight, a "ruction" is a free-for-all and a "noggin" is a small mug or cup. And "Thanum an dial" (pronounced tannum-an-dale) means soul of the devil.

Circa 1850
Traditional

AD LIB

Tim Fin-ne-gan lived in Wat-lin' Street, A gen-tle-man Ir-ish,

might-y odd. He'd a beau-ti-ful brogue so rich and sweet And to

rise in the world he car-ried a hod. You see, he'd a sort of the

tip-plin' way, With the love for the li-quor poor Tim was born. To

help him on with his work each day He'd a drop of the crea-tur ev'-ry morn.

Whack fol the da now, dance to your part-ner, Welt the floor, your trot-ters shake.

Was-n't it the truth I told you— Lots of fun at Fin-ne-gan's Wake.

Tim Finnegan lived in Watlin' Street,
A gentleman Irish, mighty odd.
He'd a beautiful brogue so rich and sweet
And to rise in the world he carried a hod.
You see, he'd a sort of the tipplin' way,
With the love for the liquor poor Tim was born.
To help him on with his work each day
He'd a drop o' the creatur ev'ry morn.

CHORUS:
> Whack fol the da now, dance to your partner,
> Welt the floor, your trotters shake.
> Wasn't it the truth I told you—
> Lots of fun at Finnegan's Wake.

One mornin' Tim was rather full,
His head felt heavy which made him shake;
He fell from a ladder and he broke his skull,
And they carried him home, his corpse to wake.
They rolled him up in a nice clean sheet,
And laid him out upon the bed—
With a gallon of whisky at his feet,
And a barrel of porter at his head! *CHORUS:*

His friends assembled at the wake
And Mrs Finnegan called for lunch.
First they brought in tay and cake,
Then pipes, tobacco and whisky punch.
Biddy O'Brien began to cry,
"Such a nice clean corpse did you ever see?
Ah, Tim, mavourneen, why did you die?"
"Arrah, shut you gob!" said Paddy McGhee.
CHORUS:

Then Maggie O'Conner took up the job:
"Oh, Biddy," said she, "you're wrong, I'm sure."
Biddy gave her a belt in the gob,
And left her sprawlin' on the floor.
Then the war did soon engage —
'Twas woman to woman, and man to man;
Shillelagh law was all the rage
And a row and a ruction soon began.
CHORUS:

Mickey Maloney raised his head
When a noggin of whisky flew at him;
It missed, and fallin' on the bed,
The liquor scattered over Tim.
Tim revives! See how he rises!
Tim Finnegan risin' from the bed,
Sayin', "Whirl your whisky around like blazes,
Thanum an dial, do you think I'm dead?"
CHORUS (twice!):

The Parting Glass

The parting glass is a metaphor for life's bittersweet leave-takings. As such, this song has become a traditional closing number for, most notably, The Clancy Brothers.

FREELY   Traditional

O,— all the mon-ey that e're I spent, I— spent it in— good—

com - pan - y, And— all the harm— that e're I've done, A -

las it was— to— none but me. And all— I've— done for

want— of— wit To mem - 'ry now I— can't re- call. So—

fill to me— the par - ting glass, Good - night and joy— be— with you all.

O, all the money that e're I spent,
I spent it in good company,
And all the harm that e're I've done,
Alas it was to none but me.
And all I've done for want of wit
To mem'ry now I can't recall.
So fill to me the parting glass,
Good-night, and joy be with you all.

If I had money enough to spend,
And leisure time to sit awhile,
There is a fair maid in this town
That sorely has my heart beguiled.
Her rosy cheeks and ruby lips—
I own she has my heart in thrall.
So fill to me the parting glass,
Good night, and joy be with you all.

O, all the comrades that e're I had
Are sorry for my going away,
And all the sweethearts that e're I had
Would wish me one more day to stay.
But since it falls unto my lot
That I should rise and you should not,
I'll gently rise and softly call,
Good night, and joy be with you all.

PART TWO

MEN & WOMEN,
LOVE & WAR

Maid of the Sweet Brown Knowe

This tune humorously represents the ebb and flow of courting, in which first one and then the other party seems to take the advantage. A "knowe" is a hill or hummock of land.

AT A LIVELY CLIP

Traditional

Oh,— come all ye lads— and las - sies and lis - ten to me a while,— And I'll sing for you a verse or two that will cause you all to smile.— It's all a-bout a fair young man, and I'm go - ing to tell you now— How he late - ly came— a - court - in' of the maid of the sweet brown knowe.

Oh, come all ye lads and lassies and listen to me a while,
And I'll sing for you a verse or two that will cause you all to smile.
It's all about a fair young man, and I'm goin' to tell you now
How he lately came a-courtin' of the maid of the sweet brown knowe.

Said he, "My pretty fair maid, will you come along with me?
We'll both go off together and it's married we will be.
We'll join our hands in wedlock bands, I'm speakin' to you now;
And I'll do my best endeavor for the maid of the sweet brown knowe."

This fair and fickle young thing, she knew not what to say;
Her eyes did shine like silver bright and merrily did play.
Said she, "Young man, your love subdue, for I'm not ready now;
And I'll spend another season at the foot of the sweet brown knowe."

Said he, "My pretty fair maid, how can you answer so?
Look down on yonder valley where my verdant crops do grow.
Look down on yonder valley, where horses, men and plough
Are at their daily labor for the maid of the sweet brown knowe."

"If they're at their daily labor, kind sir, it is not for me.
For I've heard of your behavior; I have, indeed," said she.
"There is an inn where you call in, I've heard the people say,
Where you rap and you call, and pay for all, and go home at the break of day."

"If I rap and I call, and I pay for all, the money is all my own,
And I'll never spend your fortune, for I hear that you have none.
You thought you had my poor heart broke in talkin' with me now,
But I'll leave you where I found you, at the foot of the sweet brown knowe."

Well, now, ye lads and lassies, you've listened to me a while,
And I've sung for you a verse or two; I hope they made you smile.
'Twas all about a fair young man, what I've told you now,
And how he lately came a-courtin' of the maid of the sweet brown knowe.

Larry Mick McGarry

The multi-talented Percy French (1854-1920) was a painter as well as a songwriter and performer. He became one of Ireland's most beloved troubadours as he pedaled his bicycle from town to town. This delightful song, the last he wrote, is in dialect, as are many of his humorous tunes.

SPRIGHTLY

Words and music by Percy French, 1915

O! Lar-ry Mick Mc-Gar-ry was the tor-ment of the town,_____ A

lad a wo-man's glad o' but a man would like to drown._____ With a

smile he would be-guile a-way a girl_____ from her boy,_____ An' be-

fore he got a mile a-way he tir-ed of his toy._____

CHORUS:

Tith-er-y-ah the doo-dle ah, no mar-ry-in' for me!_____

Tith-er-y-ah the doo-dle ah, as far as I can see._____

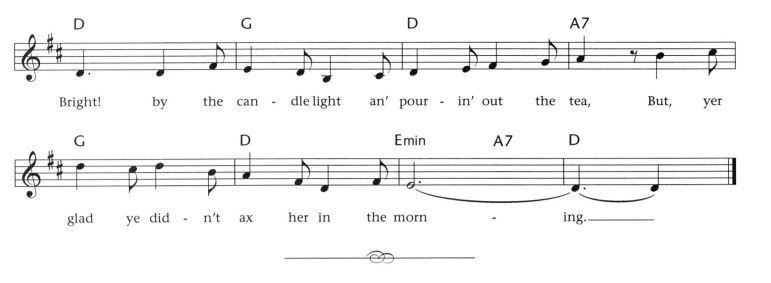

Bright! by the can - dle light an' pour - in' out the tea, But, yer
glad ye did - n't ax her in the morn - ing._____

O! Larry Mick McGarry was the torment of the town,
A lad a woman's glad o' but a man would like to drown.
With a smile he would beguile away a girl from her boy,
An' before he got a mile away he tired of his toy.

CHORUS: Tith-er-y-ah the doodle ah, no marryin' for me!
            Tith-er-y-ah the doodle ah, as far as I can see.
            Bright! by the candle light an' pourin' out the tea,
            But, yer glad ye didn't ax her in the morning.

O, Larry played old Harry with the girls about the place,
At the dancin' they'd be glancin' at the features of his face;
But he never would endeavour to be lover-like until
Mary Carey, she's a fairy, had him goin' like a mill.

CHORUS: Tith-er-y-ah the doodle ah, he met her in the street;
            Tith-er-y-ah the doodle ah, sez he, "Yer lookin' sweet.
            A walk an' a talk wid you I think would be a treat."
            But all he got from Mary was, "Good morning!"

The dancin' down at Clancy's brought in all the neighbourhood,
Though the roof wasn't waterproof, the floor was fairly good;
An' Larry Mick McGarry he could handle well the leg,
But Mary, light an' airy, O! she took him down a peg.

CHORUS: Tith-er-y-ah the doodle ah, she footed it wid Flynn
            Tith-er-y-ah the doodle ah, an' all the other min.
            But Larry Mick McGarry, O! he hadn't a look in;
            Faith, he had to go and find her in the morning.

O, she taught him 'til she brought him up to where she had designed;
Sez Larry, "Will ye marry me?" Sez she, "I wouldn't mind."
He kissed her an' carissed her which is quite the proper thing
Then together, hell for leather, they were off to buy a ring.

CHORUS: Tith-er-y-ah the doodle ah, "No marryin'," sez you!
            Tith-er-y-ah the doodle ah, ye may escape the 'flu.
            Wait 'til you meet yer mate an' all there is to do
            Is to go an' buy the licence in the morning.

Three Lovely Lassies from Kimmage

Kimmage is a suburban area of Dublin, but there are versions of this song from other towns as well. A "T.D." is a member of Ireland's parliament, the Dáil, and "da" is dialectic for dad.

BOASTFULLY   Traditional

There were three love-ly las-sies from Kim-mage, From Kim-mage,

from Kim-mage; And when-e'er was a bit of a scrim-mage,

Sure, I was the tough-est of all, Sure, I was the tough-est of all.

There were three lovely lassies from Kimmage,
From Kimmage, from Kimmage;
And whene'er was a bit of a scrimmage,
Sure, I was the toughest of all,
Sure, I was the toughest of all.

Well, the cause of the row was Joe Cashin,
Joe Cashin, Joe Cashin;
For he told me he thought I looked smashin'
At a dance at the Adelaide Hall,
At a dance at the Adelaide Hall.

Now, the other two lassies were flippin',
Were flippin', were flippin';
When they saw me and me Joe go trippin'
To the strains of the Tennessee Waltz,
To the strains of the Tennessee Waltz.

When he gets a few jars he goes frantic,
Goes frantic, goes frantic;
But he's tall and he's dark and romantic,
And I love him in spite of it all,
And I love him in spite of it all.

He told me he thought we should marry,
Should marry, should marry;
He said it was foolish to tarry,
So, I lent him the price of a ring,
So, I lent him the price of a ring.

Well, me da said he'd give us a present,
A present, a present:
A stool and a lovely stuffed pheasant,
And a picture to hang on the wall,
And a picture to hang on the wall.

I went down to the tenancy section,
The section, the section;
The T.D. just before the election,
Said he'd get me a house near me ma,
Said he'd get me a house near me ma.

Well I'm getting a house, the man said it,
Man said it, man said it,
When I've five or six kids to me credit;
In the meantime we'll live with me ma,
In the meantime we'll live with me ma.

Reilly's Daughter

Old Reilly sounds like quite a difficult character, with his one glittering red eye and his "mind for murder and slaughter." The fact that he plays on "the big bass drum" suggests that he is one of Northern Ireland's militant Protestants who lead marches of the like-minded through Catholic neighborhoods each July pounding on huge drums in celebration of Protestant victories over the Catholics more than 300 years ago. Of course, painting him so luridly is greatly to our hero's credit when he vanquishes the old devil with relative ease. A "scratch" is something thrown together hastily.

RECKLESSLY   Traditional

As I was sit-ting by the fire Eat-ing spuds and— drink-ing port-er,

Sud-den-ly a thought came in-to my head: I'd like to mar-ry old

Reil-ly's daugh-ter! Gid-dy-i-ay, gid-dy-i-ay, gid-dy-i-ay for the

one-eyed Reil-ly, Gid-dy-i-ay, bang-bang-bang! Play it on your big bass drum!

As I was sitting by the fire
Eating spuds and drinking porter,
Suddenly a thought came into my head:
I'd like to marry old Reilly's daughter!

CHORUS: Giddy-i-ay, giddy-i-ay, giddy-i-ay for the one-eyed Reilly,
                  Giddy-i-ay, *bang!-bang!-bang!*
                  Play it on your big bass drum!

For Reilly played on the big bass drum,
Reilly had a mind for murder and slaughter;
Reilly had a bright red glittering eye
And he kept that eye on his lovely daughter.   *CHORUS:*

Her hair was black and her eyes were blue,
The colonel and the major and the captain sought her;
The sergeant and the private and the drummer boy, too,
But they never had a chance with old Reilly's daughter.   *CHORUS:*

I got me a ring and a parson, too,
I got me a scratch in the married quarter,
Settled me down to a peaceful life
Happy as a king with old Reilly's daughter.   *CHORUS:*

Suddenly a footstep on the stair,
Who should it be but Reilly out for slaughter,
With two pistols in his hands,
Looking for the man who had stolen his daughter.   *CHORUS:*

I caught old Reilly by the hair,
Rammed his head in a pail of water,
Fired his pistols into the air,
A darned sight quicker than I married his daughter.   *CHORUS:*

The Zoological Gardens

The Zoological Gardens, located in Dublin's famous Phoenix Park, here include not only the zoo itself, but also some of the shady and secluded areas of the park one passes through in order to get there, favored by generations of lovers for "monkey business"!

LIGHTHEARTED   *Traditional*

Oh, thun - der and light - ning is___ no lark, When Dub - lin

Cit - y is in___ the dark. If you have an - y mon - ey go

up to the Park And view the Zoo - lo - gi - cal Gar - dens.

Oh, thunder and lightning is no lark,
When Dublin City is in the dark.
If you have any money go up to the Park
And view the Zoological Gardens.

Last Sunday night we had no dough,
So I took the mot up to see the Zoo;
We saw the lions and the kangaroos
Inside the Zoological Gardens.

Well, we went out there by Castleknock,
Said the mot to me, "Sure, we'll court by the lough."
Then I knew she was one of the rare old stock
Inside the Zoological Gardens.

Said the mot to me, "My dear friend Jack,
Sure I'd like a ride on the elephant's back."
Says I, "Cut it out or I'll give you such a crack
Inside the Zoological Gardens."

Now we went out there on our honeymoon.
Said the mot to me, "If you don't come soon
I'll have to wait with the hairy baboon
Inside the Zoological Gardens!"

Old Maid in a Garret

(I Was Told By My Aunt)

Everyone needs someone to love and to talk to. And even if that other one can't be a person, it certainly helps if it can, at least, talk back!

GAMELY   Traditional

I was told by my aunt, I was told by my moth-er, That
go-ing to a wed-ding was the mak-ing of an-oth-er; Then,
if that be so, sure, I'd go with-out a bid-ding. Oh,——
kind prov-i-dence, won't you send me to a wed-ding!

CHORUS:

And it's oh! Dear me! How will it be, If I
die an old maid in a gar - ret?

78

I was told by my aunt, I was told by my mother,
That going to a wedding was the making of another;
Then, if that be so, sure, I'd go without a bidding.
Oh, kind providence, won't you send me to a wedding!

CHORUS: And it's oh! Dear me! How will it be,
              If I die an old maid in a garret?

Now, there's my sister Jean, she's not handsome or good-looking,
Scarcely sixteen and a feller she was courting;
Now she's twenty-four, with a son and a daughter,
Here am I, forty-five, and I never had an offer.   *CHORUS:*

I can cook, I can sew, I can keep the house quite tidy;
Rise up in the morning and get the breakfast ready.
There's nothing in the whole world that makes my heart so cheery
As a wee fat man, who would call me "his own dearie."   *CHORUS:*

So, come landsman, come townsman, come tinker or come tailor,
Come fiddler, come dancer, come ploughboy or come sailor,
Come rich man, come poor man, come fool or come witty,
Come any man at all who will marry out of pity.   *CHORUS:*

Oh, well, I'm away home, for there's nobody heeding,
There's nobody heeding to poor Annie's pleading;
And I'm away home to my own wee bit garret.
If I can't get a man then I'll surely get a parrot!   *CHORUS:*

When I Was Single

Every relationship is unique, and different people have their different ways of making things work out to their satisfaction. The following five songs highlight five women with different situations, and illustrate a whole spectrum of solutions. The first shows that true love can be very forgiving, indeed.

BROADLY   *Traditional*

When I was sin - gle I wore a plaid shawl, But___ now that I'm mar - ried I wear none at all. Ah! but still I love him,___ I'll for - give him.___ I'll go with him___ where - ev - er he goes.

When I was single I wore a plaid shawl,
But now that I'm married I wear none at all.

CHORUS: Ah! but still I love him,
               I'll forgive him.
               I'll go with him wherever he goes.

He came up our alley and he whistled me out,
But the tail of his shirt from the trousers hung out.   *CHORUS:*

He bought me a handkerchief, red, white and blue,
But before I could wear it, he tore it in two.   *CHORUS:*

He brought me to an ale-house and he bought me some stout,
But before I could drink it, he ordered me out.   *CHORUS:*

He borrowed some money to buy me a ring;
Then he and the jeweller went off on a fling.   *CHORUS:*

There's cakes in the oven, there's cheese on the shelf.
If you want any more, you can sing it yourself.   *CHORUS:*

Never Wed an Old Man

(Maids, When You're Young)

There is no substitute for experience. But, what does one do when one realizes one's mistake? Though this song can be performed in tempo throughout, the impact can be increased significantly by singing the verses freely and with emphasis.

KNOWINGLY

Traditional

An old man came court-in' me, hey ding door-um di. An old man came court-in' me, me be-in' young. An old man came court-in' me, want-ed to mar-ry me, Maids, when you're young nev-er wed an old man.

CHORUS:

For he's got no fal-or-um, fal-did-dle-i-or-um, He's got no fal-or-um, fal-did-dle-di-day; He's got no fal-or-um, he's lost his ding dor-um! Maids, when you're young nev-er wed an old man.

An old man came courtin' me, hey ding doorum di.
An old man came courtin' me, me bein' young.
An old man came courtin' me, wanted to marry me.
Maids, when you're young never wed an old man.

CHORUS: For he's got no falorum, fal-diddle-i-orum,
              He's got no falorum, fal-diddle-di-day;
              He's got no falorum, he's lost his ding dorum!
              Maids, when you're young never wed an old man.

When we went to church, hey ding doorum di.
When we went to church, me bein' young.
When we went to church, he left me in the lurch.
Maids, when you're young never wed an old man.   *CHORUS:*

When we went to bed, hey ding doorum di.
When we went to bed, me bein' young.
When we went to bed, he lay there like he was dead.
Maids, when you're young never wed an old man.   *CHORUS:*

When this old man goes to sleep, hey ding doorum di.
When this old man goes to sleep, me bein' young.
When this old man goes to sleep, out of bed I do creep,
Into the arms of a handsome young man.

CHORUS (modified):   For he's got his falorum, fal-diddle-i-orum,
                        He's got his falorum, fal-diddle-di-day;
                        He's got his falorum, he found my ding dorum!
                        Maids, when you're young never wed an old man.

A young man is my delight, hey ding a doorum di.
A young man is my delight, me bein' young.
A young man is my delight, he'll kiss you day and night.
Maids, when you're young never wed an old man.   *CHORUS (modified as above):*

The German Clockwinder

This young lady from Grosvenor Square would surely agree that there is a great deal to be said for hiring the right man for the job.

MIT OOMPH!

Traditional

A Ger - man clock - wind - er to Dub - lin once came, Ben - ja - min

Fooks was the bould Ger - man's name; And as he was wind - ing his

way 'round the Strand He played on his flute and the mu - sic was grand.

CHORUS:

Sing - ing too - ra - lum - ma - lum - ma, too - ra - lum - ma - lum - ma, too - ra - lie - ay, Too - ra - lie,

too - ra - lie, you - ra - lie - ay, Too - ra - lum - ma - lum - ma, too - ra - lum - ma - lum - ma,

too - ra - lie - ay, Too - ra - lie, you - ra - lie, you - ra - lie - ay.

A German clockwinder to Dublin once came,
Benjamin Fooks was the bould German's name;
And as he was winding his way 'round the Strand
He played on his flute and the music was grand.

CHORUS: Singing too-ra-lumma-lumma, too-ra-lumma-lumma, too-ra-lie-ay,
Too-ra-lie, too-ra-lie, you-ra-lie-ay,
Too-ra-lumma-lumma, too-ra-lumma-lumma, too-ra-lie-ay,
Too-ra-lie, you-ra-lie, you-ra-lie-ay.

O, there was a young lady from Grosvenor Square
Who said that her clock was in need of repair.
In walks the bould German and, to her delight,
In less than five minutes he had her clock right.   *CHORUS:*

Now as they were settled down there on the floor,
There came this very loud knock on the door.
In walked her husband and great was his shock
For to see the bould German wind up his wife's clock.   *CHORUS:*

The husband, says he, "Now look here, Mary Anne,
Don't let that bould German come in here again.
He wound up your clock and left mine on the shelf;
If your oul' clock needs winding, sure, I'll wind it meself!"   *CHORUS:*

Quare Bungle Rye

Caveat emptor! Both "begorrah" and "bedad" are mild Irish oaths, euphemisms for God.

RYE-LY   *Traditional*

Now, Jack was a sail - or who roamed on the town, And
she was a dam - sel who skipped up and down. Said the dam - sel to
Jack,— as she passed him by, "Would you care for to
pur - chase some quare bun - gle rye, rod - dy rye?"
Fol the did-dle rye, rod - dy rye, rod - dy rye._____

Now, Jack was a sailor who roamed on the town,
And she was a damsel who skipped up and down.
Said the damsel to Jack, as she passed him by,
"Would you care for to purchase some quare bungle rye, roddy rye?"
          Fol the diddle rye, roddy rye, roddy rye.

Thought Jack to himself, now what can this be,
But the finest of whisky from far Germany,
Smuggled up in a basket and sold on the sly,
And the name that it goes by is Quare bungle rye, roddy rye.
          Fol the diddle rye, roddy rye, roddy rye.

Jack gave her a pound and he thought nothing strange;
Said she, "Hold the basket 'til I get you your change."
Jack looked in the basket and a baby did spy.
"Oh, Begorrah," said Jack, "This is quare bungle rye, roddy rye!"
          Fol the diddle rye, roddy rye, roddy rye.

Jack looked for her to return, but in vain,
She had skipped and he never saw her again.
And it wasn't too long, 'til the babe 'gan to cry.
"To be sure," said Jack, "This is quare bungle rye, roddy rye!"
          Fol the diddle rye, roddy rye, roddy rye.

Now to get the child christened was Jack's first intent,
For to get the child christened to the parson he went.
Said the parson to Jack, "What name will he go by?"
"Bedad, now," said Jack, "Call him Quare Bungle Rye, roddy rye."
          Fol the diddle rye, roddy rye roddy rye.

Said the parson to Jack, "Now that's a queer name."
Said Jack to the parson, "It's a queer way he came,
Smuggled up in a basket and sold on the sly,
And the name that he'll go by is Quare Bungle Rye, roddy rye."
          Fol the diddle rye, roddy rye, roddy rye.

Now all you young sailors who roam on the town
Beware of those damsels who skip up and down.
Take a look in their baskets as they pass you by,
Or else they might sell you some quare bungle rye, roddy rye.
          Fol the diddle rye, roddy rye, roddy rye.

The Old Woman From Wexford

This old woman's solution to her conflict of interests doesn't quite work out as she had planned.

BRASHLY

Traditional

Oh, there was an old wo - man from Wex - ford, And in Wex - ford she did

dwell, She loved her old man dear - ly, But an - oth-er man twice as well.

CHORUS:

With me rum - dom-dom - dom di - ro, And me rum - dom-dom di - ree.

Oh, there was an old woman from Wexford,
And in Wexford she did dwell,
She loved her old man dearly,
But another man twice as well.

CHORUS: With me rum-dom-dom-dom di-ro,
                      And me rum-dom-dom di-ree.

One day she went to the doctor,
Some medicine for to find,
Saying, "Doctor, will you give me somethin'
For to make me old man blind?"   CHORUS:

"Oh, feed him eggs and marrowbones
And make him suck them all,
And it won't be very long after
'Til he won't see you at all."   CHORUS:

Then the doctor wrote a letter,
He signed it with his hand,
And he sent it 'round to the old man,
Just to let him understand.   CHORUS:

She fed him eggs and marrowbones
And made him suck them all,
And it wasn't very long after 'til
He couldn't see the wall.   CHORUS:

"Oh," says he, "I'd go and drown meself,
But that might be a sin."
"Well," says she, "I'll go along with you
And help to push you in."   CHORUS:

The woman she stepped back a bit
To get a running go,
But the old man blithely stepped aside
And she went tumblin' in below.   CHORUS:

Oh, how loudly she did roar
And how loudly she did bawl.
"Arrah, hold your whist, old woman!" says he,
"Sure, I can't see you at all."   CHORUS:

Now eggs are eggs and marrowbones
May make your old man blind,
But if you want to drown him
You must creep up close behind.   CHORUS:

The Cobbler

In this song, popularized in recent years by Tommy Makem, it is the husband's solution that has the wife once again ending up in the water. A "lapstone" is just what the word says—a stone or iron plate held in the lap on which a shoemaker hammers leather.

RAKISHLY   Traditional

Oh, they call me Dick Dar - by, I'm a cob - bler, I

served me time at Old Camp._____ Some say I'm an old ag - i -

ta - tor, But now I'm re - solved to re - pent.

CHORUS:

With me ing - twing of an ing - thing of an i - day, With me

ing - twing of an ing - thing of an i - day, With me roo - boo - boo roo - boo - boo

ran - dy, And me lap - stone keeps beat - in' a - way.

Oh, they call me Dick Darby, I'm a cobbler,
I served me time at Old Camp.
Some say I'm an old agitator,
But now I'm resolved to repent.

CHORUS: With me ing-twing of an ing-thing of an i-day,
                   With me ing-twing of an ing-thing of an i-day,
                   With me roo-boo-boo roo-boo-boo randy,
                   And me lapstone keeps beatin' away.

Now, me father was hung for sheep stealing,
Me mother was burned for a witch;
Me sister's a dandy house-keeper,
And I'm a mechanical switch.   *CHORUS:*

Ah, it's forty long years I have travelled
All by the contents of me pack;
Me hammers, me awls and me pinchers,
I carry them all on me back.   *CHORUS:*

Oh, me wife she is humpy, she's lumpy,
Me wife she's the devil in black!
And no matter what I may do with her,
Her tongue it goes clickety-clack.   *CHORUS:*

So, early one fine summer's morning,
A little before it was day,
I dipped her three times in the river
And carelessly bade her, "Good Day!"   *CHORUS:*

The Twang Man

This old broadsheet ballad is sometimes attributed to Michael J. Moran, also known as Zozimus, a blind Dublin balladeer of the early 19th century, and may well memorialize an actual murder. It is set to the tune of Limerick is Beautiful. The definition of "Twang" in this context is uncertain, but The Oxford English Dictionary indicates that it is an old Australian slang term for opium. "Traycle" is dialectic for treacle, a molasses sweetener.

MODERATELY

Words attributed to Zozimus (Michael J. Moran)
Air is Limerick is Beautiful

Come Listen to me story, 'Tis 'bout a nice young man. When the Mil - i - tia was - n't want - tin' He dealt in hawk - in' Twang. He loved a love - ly maid - den, As fair as a - ny midge. An' she kep' a tray - cle de - pot Wan side of the Car - lisle Bridge.

Come listen to me story,
'Tis 'bout a nice young man.
When the militia wasn't wantin'
He dealt in hawkin' Twang.
He loved a lovely maiden,
As fair as any midge.
An' she kep' a traycle depot
Wan side of the Carlisle Bridge.

Another wan came a-coortin' her,
His name was Mickey Bags;
He was a commercial traveller
An' he dealt in bones and rags.
Well, he took her out to Sandymount
For to see the waters rowl,
An' he stole the heart of the Twang man's girl
Playin' Billy-in-the-Bowl!

Oh, when the Twang man heard of that
He flew into a terrible rage,
An' he swore be the contents of his Twang cart
On him he'd have revenge.
So, he stood in wait near James' gate
'Til the poor old Bags came up;
With his Twang knife, sure, he tuk the lief
Of the poor ould gather-em-up!

Weile Waile

This grisly little ballad started as a children's song. Isn't it odd how many nursery rhymes and fairy tales from diverse lands refer to mayhem and death?

WITH PERVERSE ZEST   *Traditional*

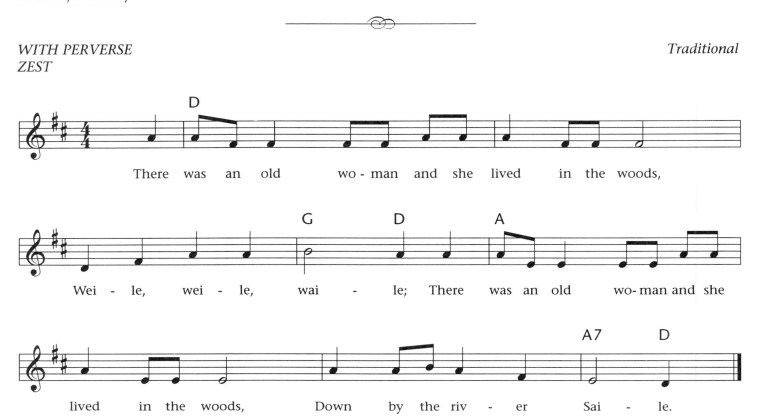

There was an old wo-man and she lived in the woods,

Wei - le, wei - le, wai - le; There was an old wo-man and she

lived in the woods, Down by the riv - er Sai - le.

There was an old woman and she lived in the woods,
Weile, weile, waile;
There was an old woman and she lived in the woods,
Down by the river Saile.

She had a baby, six months old,
Weile, weile, waile;
She had a baby, six months old,
Down by the river Saile.

She had a pen-knife, three foot long,
Weile, weile, waile;
She had a pen-knife, three foot long,
Down by the river Saile.

She stuck the pen-knife in the baby's heart,
Weile, weile, waile;
She stuck the pen-knife in the baby's heart,
Down by the river Saile.

Three detective bobbies came knocking at the door,
Weile, weile, waile;
Three detective bobbies came knocking at the door,
Down by the river Saile.

"Are you the woman who killed the child?"
Weile, weile, waile;
"Are you the woman who killed the child?"
Down by the river Saile.

"Yes, I'm the woman who killed the child."
Weile, weile, waile;
"Yes, I'm the woman who killed the child."
Down by the river Saile.

The rope got chucked and she was hung,
Weile, weile, waile;
The rope got chucked and she was hung,
Down by the river Saile.

And that was the end of the woman in the woods,
Weile, weile, waile;
And that was the end of the woman in the woods,
Down by the river Saile.

Nell (Ned) Flaherty's Drake

One woman's (or man's) meat is another woman's (or man's) beloved. This tale of murder most fowl reminds us that there is no greater love than that of a woman (or man) for her (or his) duck! A "hake" is a fish, similar to a cod.

RIGHTEOUSLY

Traditional

O! Me name it is Nell, and the truth for to tell,— I come from Coote Hill, which I'll nev-er de-ny. I— had a fine drake, and I'd die for his sake, That me grand-moth-er left me and she goin' to die. The dear lit-tle fel-low, his legs, they were yel-low, He could fly like a swal-low and swim like a hake. 'Til some dirt-y sav-age, to graise his white cab-bage, Most wan-ton-ly mur-dered me beau-ti-ful drake.

O! Me name it is Nell (Ned), and the truth for to tell (I have said),
I come from Coote Hill, which I'll never deny.
I had a fine drake, and I'd die for his sake,
That me grandmother left me and she goin' to die.
The dear little fellow, his legs, they were yellow,
He could fly like a swallow and swim like a hake.
'Til some dirty savage, to graise his white cabbage,
Most wantonly murdered me beautiful drake.

His neck it was green, O, most fit to be seen;
He was fit for a queen of the highest degree.
His body was white and it would you delight,
He was plump, fat and heavy, and brisk as a bee.
He was wholesome and sound, he would weigh twenty pound,
And the universe round I would roam for his sake.
Bad wind to the robber—be he drunk or sober—
That murdered Nell (Ned) Flaherty's beautiful drake!

May his pig never grunt, may his cat never hunt,
May a ghost ever haunt in the dead of the night;
May his hens never lay, may his ass never bray,
May his goat fly away like an old paper kite!
That the flies and the fleas may that wretch ever tease,
May the piercin' March breeze make him shiver and shake;
May a lump of a stick raise the bumps fast and thick
On the monster that murdered Nell (Ned) Flaherty's drake!

May his spade never dig, may his sow never pig,
May each hair in his wig be well thrashed with the flail;
May his door never latch, may his roof have no thatch,
May his turkeys not hatch, may the rats eat his mail!
May ev'ry old Fairy from Cork to Dunleary
Dip him snug and airy in river or lake,
Where the eel and the trout, they may dine on the snout
Of the monster that murdered Nell (Ned) Flaherty's drake!

Now the only good news that I have to infuse
Is that old Paddy Hughes and young Anthony Blake,
Also Johnny Dwyer and Corney Maguire—
They each have a grandson of me darlin' drake.
Me treasure had dozens of nephews and cousins
And one I must get or me heart it will brake.
For to set me mind aisy, or else I'll run crazy!
So ends the whole song of Nell (Ned) Flaherty's drake!

I'll Tell Me Ma

This is a children's skipping song from Belfast, popular with pub bands.

PLAYFULLY

Traditional

I'll tell me ma, when I go home, The boys won't leave the girls a - lone. They

pulled my hair and they stole my comb, Well, that's al - right 'til I go home.

She is hand-some, she is pret - ty, She is the belle of Bel - fast Cit - y.

She is a-court - in', one, two, three, Please, won't you tell me who is she?

I'll tell me ma, when I go home,
The boys won't leave the girls alone.
They pulled my hair and they stole my comb,
Well, that's alright 'til I go home.
She is handsome, she is pretty,
She is the belle of Belfast City.
She is a-courtin', one, two, three,
Please, won't you tell me who is she?

Albert Mooney is fighting for her,
All the boys, they swear they'll have her.
They rap at the door and they ring at the bell,
Saying, "Oh, my true love, are you well?"
Out she comes, as white as snow,
Rings on her fingers and bells on her toes.
Old Jenny Murray says she'll die
If she doesn't get the fellow with the roving eye.

Let the wind and the rain and the hail blow high,
And the snow come tumbling from the sky.
She's as nice as apple pie,
She'll get her own lad by and by.
When she gets a lad all of her own,
She won't tell her ma when she gets home.
Let them all say as they will,
For it's Albert Mooney loves her still.

(Optional: Repeat first verse)

The Fortunes of Finnegan

Percy French, again writing a humorous song in dialect, has managed a wonderful fusion of rhyming Irish names into the rhythm of the language. "M.P." stands for a Member of Parliament, and "crass" is a dialectic shortening of crossroads, where country folk would often meet and greet and catch up on the latest local news.

Words by Percy French
Music by Houston Collisson, a pastor
Circa 1900

WITH HUMOR

'Twas Bran - a - gan an' Flan - a - gan were talk - in' at the "crass," When

up comes Lar - ry Lan - a - gan a - driv - in' of an ass. Says

he, "Poor Pe - ter Fin - ne - gan is laid out migh - ty flat— While

rea - dy - in' his sup - per he was bit - ten by the cat."

CHORUS:

Says Bran - a - gan to Flan - a - gan, an' Flan - a - gan to Lan - a - gan,

"Lit - tle Pe - ter Fin - ne - gan will not get ov - er that." But

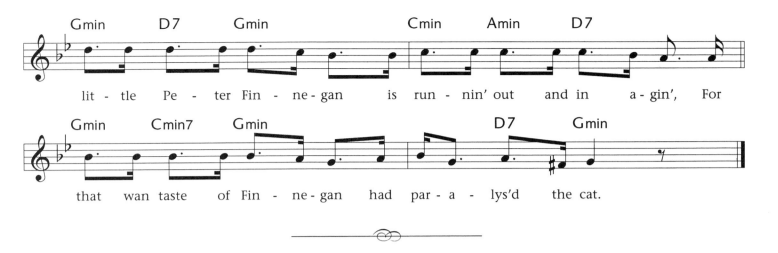

lit - tle Pe - ter Fin - ne - gan is run - nin' out and in a - gin', For that wan taste of Fin - ne - gan had par - a - lys'd the cat.

'Twas Branagan an' Flanagan were talkin' at the "crass,"
When up comes Larry Lanagan a-drivin' of an ass.
Says he, "Poor Peter Finnegan is laid out mighty flat—
While readyin' his supper he was bitten by the cat."

CHORUS: Says Branagan to Flanagan, an' Flanagan to Lanagan,
    "Little Peter Finnegan will not get over that."
    But little Peter Finnegan is runnin' out an' in agin',
    For that wan taste of Finnegan had paralys'd the cat.

When Peter grew up big an' brown, a blacksmith he was made,
An' not a man in all the town could beat him at his trade.
One day to chase some corner boys he rushed out of his shed.
A motor-car was passin' an' it struck him on the head.

CHORUS: Says Branagan to Flanagan, an' Flanagan to Lanagan,
    "I hear that Peter Finnegan has gone to glory clean."
    But brawny Peter Finnegan's a horrid man to run agin—
    They found that Peter Finnegan was mendin' the machine.

The boys in all the Barony were courtin' Mary Flynn,
And no one but that Finnegan would have a chance to win.
All the others when they'd meet her 'bout the dowry would begin;
"But I'll take you, girl," says Peter, "in the clothes you're standin' in!"

CHORUS: Says Branagan to Flanagan, an' Flanagan to Lanagan,
    "It isn't Peter Finnegan she'll honour an' obey."
    But sorra a man but Finnegan will flirt wid Mary Flynn agin,
    For bruisin' Peter Finnegan she married yesterday.

'Twas politics that Finnegan would study day an' night;
He'd argue right was mostly wrong an' black was really white.
And when the next election came the posters on the wall
Read, "Vote for Peter Finnegan and the divil a tax at all!"

CHORUS: Says Branagan to Flanagan, an' Flanagan to Lanagan,
    "The vote that Peter votes himself his only vote will be."
    But Finnegan can win agin, no matter who he's in agin',
    And bruisin' Peter Finnegan is Finnegan M.P.

Mush, Mush, Mush Tu-Ral-I-Ady

In the classic film, The Quiet Man, *the convivial singers omit the second ending of the verse and go right into "Mush, mush." Thus, the last word is in parentheses. The Shannon is the longest river in Ireland, flowing south from its source in the mountains of County Cavan to Limerick Town, where it turns west to the Atlantic Ocean. A "boreen" is a narrow country path, and a "woodbine" is a twining shrub, like a honeysuckle.*

BLARNEY, STONED

Traditional

It was there I learned read-in' and writ-in',___ At Dick Cro-ly's where
(Him and) me we had ma-ny a scrim-mage,___ And div-il a

I went to school.___ And 'twas there I learned howl-in' and__ fight-in'
co-py I wrote;___ There was nev-er a gos-soon in the vil-age

With me school-mas-ter Mis-ter O' Toole.___ Him and
Dared tread on the tail of me

OPTIONAL: SKIP RIGHT TO CHORUS.
(coat.)___

CHORUS:

Mush, mush, mush tu-ral-i-ad-y,___ Sing mush, mush, mush tur-ral-i-

ay.___ There was nev-er a gos-soon in the vil-lage

Dared tread on the tail of me coat.

It was there I learned readin' and writin',
At Dick Croly's where I went to school.
And 'twas there I learned howlin' and fightin'
With me schoolmaster Mister O'Toole.
Him and me we had many a scrimmage,
And divil a copy I wrote;
There was never a gossoon in the village
Dared tread on the tail of me (coat).

CHORUS: Mush, mush, mush tu-ral-i-ady,
Sing mush, mush, mush tu-ral-i-ay.
There was never a gossoon in the village
Dared tread on the tail of me coat.

O 'twas there I learned all of me courtin',
Many lessons I took in the art;
'Til Cupid, the blackguard, while sportin',
An arrow drove straight thro' me heart.
Molly O'Connor, she lived down the boreen,
And tender lines to her I wrote.
If you dare say one hard word agin' her,
I'll tread on the tail of your (coat).

CHORUS: Mush, mush, mush tu-ral-i-ady,
Sing mush, mush, mush tu-ral-i-ay.
If you dare say one hard word agin' her,
I'll tread on the tail of your coat.

But a rascal called Mickey Maloney
Came and stole her affections away,
For he'd money, and I hadn't any,
So, I sent him a challenge next day.
In the evening we met at the woodbine,
The Shannon we crossed in a boat,
And I lathered him with me shillelagh
For he trod on the tail of me (coat).

CHORUS: Mush, mush, mush tu-ral-i-ady,
Sing mush, mush, mush tu-ral-i-ay.
And I lathered him with me shillelagh
For he trod on the tail of me coat.

Oh, me fame went abroad thro' the nation,
And folks came a-flockin' to see;
And they cried out without hesitation:
"You're a fightin' man, Billy McGee!"
I have cleaned out the Finnegan faction
And I've licked all the Murphys afloat.
If you're in for a row or a ruction,
Just tread on the tail of me (coat).

CHORUS: Mush, mush, mush tu-ral-i-ady,
Sing mush, mush, mush tu-ral-i-ay.
If you're in for a row or a ruction,
Just tread on the tail of me coat.

[Optional: Repeat chorus with coat *omitted first time]*

Do You Want Your Old Lobby Washed Down?

This old song hails from County Cork and recalls those lean times when it was common practice for tenants, short of money, to offer the landlord housekeeping services in lieu of all or part of the rent. In the same way that "gossoon" is derived from the French word garçon, "Con Shine" may be a dialectic variant of concierge.

WITH A MUSIC HALL
STRUT AND SWING

Traditional

I've a nice lit - tle cot and a small bit of land And a place by the side of the sea,____ And I care a - bout no - one be - cause I be - lieve There's____ no - bo - dy cares a - bout me.____ ____ My peace is des - troyed and I'm fair - ly an - noyed By a las - sie who works in the town.____ She cries ev' - ry day as she pas - ses the way, "Do you want your old lob - by washed down?"____

CHORUS:

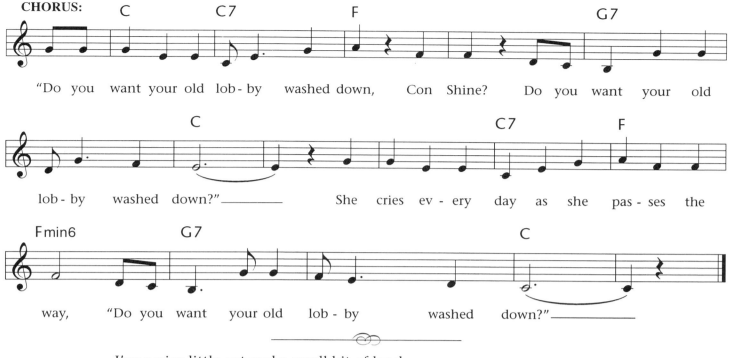

I've a nice little cot and a small bit of land
And a place by the side of the sea,
And I care about no one because I believe
There's nobody cares about me.
My peace is destroyed and I'm fairly annoyed
By a lassie who works in the town.
She cries ev'ry day as she passes the way,
"Do you want your old lobby washed down?"

CHORUS: "Do you want your old lobby washed down, Con Shine?
     Do you want your old lobby washed down?"
     She cries ev'ry day as she passes the way,
     "Do you want your old lobby washed down?"

The other day the old landlord came by for his rent;
I told him no money I had.
Besides, 'twasn't fair for to ask me to pay,
The times were so awfully bad.
He felt discontent at not getting his rent,
And he shook his big head in a frown.
Says he, "I'll take half." But says I, with a laugh,
"Do you want your old lobby washed down?"

CHORUS: "Do you want your old lobby washed down, Con Shine?
     Do you want your old lobby washed down?"
     Says he, "I'll take half." But says I, with a laugh,
     "Do you want your old lobby washed down?"

Now the boys look so bashful when they go out to court,
They seem to look so very shy;
As to kiss a young maid, sure, they seem half afraid,
But they would, if they could on the sly.
But me, I do things in a different way,
I don't give a nod or a frown.
When I go to court, I says, "Here goes for sport.
Do you want your old lobby washed down?"

CHORUS: "Do you want your old lobby washed down, Con Shine?
     Do you want your old lobby washed down?"
     When I go to court, I says, "Here goes for sport.
     "Do you want your old lobby washed down?"

The Little Beggarman

(I Am a Little Beggarman)

This little beggar considers himself a tradesman of equal stature with any other! The Liffey River runs through the center of Dublin. A "rigadoo" may refer to either the beggarman's rig, his pack of personal belongings, or, considering the melody's wonderful movement, it could be a shortened version of rigadoon, a lively dance.

NIMBLY   Traditional

Oh, I am a lit - tle beg-gar-man, a - beg - gin' I have been, For three score and more in this lit - tle Isle of Green; It's up to the Lif - fey and down to Tes - sa - gue, And I'm known by the name of the Bould John - ny Dhu. Of all the trades that's go - in', sure a - beg - gin' is the best, For when a man is tired he can sit down have a rest. He can beg for his din - ner, he has noth - in' else to do, On - ly cut a - round the cor - ner with his ould rig - a - doo.

Oh, I am a little beggarman, a-beggin' I have been,
For three score and more in this little Isle of Green;
It's up to the Liffey and down to Tessague,
And I'm known by the name of the Bould Johnny Dhu.
Of all the trades that's goin', sure a-beggin' is the best,
For when a man is tired he can sit down have a rest.
He can beg for his dinner, he has nothin' else to do,
Only cut around the corner with his ould rigadoo.

I slept one night in a barn in Currabawn,
A shockin' wet night it was, but I slept until the dawn;
There were holes in the roof and the raindrops comin' through,
And the rats and the cats were all playin' tink-a-boo.
Who did I waken but the woman of the house,
With her white-spotted apron and her fine gingham blouse;
She began to get excited and all I said was, "Boo,
Sure don't be afraid at all, 'tis only Johnny Dhu."

I met a little girl when a-walkin' out one day,
"Good morrow, little flaxy-haired girl," I did say;
"Good morrow, little beggarman, and how do you do?
With your rags and your bags and your ould rigadoo."
I'll buy a pair of leggin's and a collar and a tie,
And a nice young lady I'll go courtin' by-and-by;
I'll buy a pair of goggles and I'll color them with blue,
And an ould-fashioned lady I will make of her, too.

So all along the high road with my bag upon my back,
Over the fields with my bulgin' heavy sack;
With holes in my shoes and my toes a-peepin' through,
Singing skill-a-malick-adoodle with my ould rigadoo.
Oh, I must be goin' to bed for it's gettin' late at night,
The fire's all raked and now 'tis out the light;
For now you've heard the story of my ould rigadoo,
So it's good night and God bless you, from ould Johnny Dhu.

The Black Velvet Band

This pub favorite's lively tempo stands in sharp contrast to its warning for the unwary. Transportation was the practice, common during the first half of the 19th century, of sending convicted criminals to what was then, literally, the ends of the earth. Australia was colonized first by convicts and their captors, as was Van Diemen's Land, now called Tasmania.

WITH MERRY
RESIGNATION

Traditional
New words by Mallory & McCall

When I was a lad back in Ire- land___ Ap - pren - ticed to
('Til) bad___ mis - for - tune came o'er me___ And caused me to

trade I was bound;___ And___ be - ing an ea - ger green
go from the land,___ Far a- way from me friends and re -

coun - try boy I rel - ished the life of the town.___ 'Til
la - tions To fol - low the black vel - vet band.___

CHORUS:

Her eyes, they shone like the dia - monds,___ You'd think she was

queen of the land;___ And her hair hung o - ver her

shoul - der, Tied up with a black vel - vet band.___

When I was a lad back in Ireland
Apprenticed to trade I was bound;
And being an eager green country boy
I relished the life of the town.
'Til bad misfortune came o'er me
And caused me to go from the land,
Far away from me friends and relations
To follow the black velvet band.

CHORUS: Her eyes, they shone like the diamonds,
              You'd think she was queen of the land;
              And her hair hung over her shoulder,
              Tied up with a black velvet band.

One evening I met a fair lassie,
She swept me clean off of me feet;
We drank and we laughed in a lively pub,
I never suspected deceit.
Then, a constable came to the alehouse—
The girl slipped a watch in me hand;
"That's mine!" cried a man as she fled from me sight—
Betrayed by the black velvet band!   *CHORUS:*

They carried me off to the jailhouse
And into an iron-barred cell.
Next morning the judge looked me right in the eye
And said, "You're as guilty as hell!
And seven long years is your sentence,
Transportation to Van Dieman's Land,
Far away from your friends and relations,
You'll follow the black velvet band."   *CHORUS:*

Now, come all you jolly young fellows,
I'd have you be wary and wise;
If you meet with a frolicsome damsel, (me lads,)
Watch out for those diamond-bright eyes.
For she'll fill you with whisky and porter
'Til you are not able to stand;
And the very next thing that you'll know, (me lads,)
You've landed in Van Dieman's Land.   *CHORUS (twice):*

The Wild Colonial Boy

Isn't it remarkable how folklore seems to transform highwaymen, bandits and others who hold themselves "above the law" so they emerge as latter day Robin Hoods! Unlike the hapless hero of The Black Velvet Band, *Jack Duggan appears to have chosen to emigrate of his own volition—by the second half of the 19th century, the practice of sentencing criminals to transportation had been abolished. Castlemaine is in County Kerry, about five miles northeast of Dingle Bay.*

WITH SPIRIT

Traditional
Mid- to late-19th century

CHORUS:

There was a wild co - lo - nial boy, Jack Dug-gan was his name.____ ____ He was born and raised in Ire - land in a place called Cas - tle - maine.____ ____ He was his fa - ther's on - ly son, his moth - er's pride and joy;____ And dear - ly did his par - ents love the wild co - lo - nial boy.____

VERSE:

At the ear - ly age of six - teen years he left his na - tive home.____ ____ And to Aus - tra - lia's sun - ny land he__ was in - clined to roam.____

He robbed the rich and he helped the poor; his foes he did de-stroy.

But nev - er hurt a good man did the wild co - lo - nial boy.

CHORUS: There was a wild colonial boy, Jack Duggan was his name.
He was born and raised in Ireland in a place called Castlemaine.
He was his father's only son, his mother's pride and joy;
And dearly did his parents love the wild colonial boy.

At the early age of sixteen years he left his native home
And to Australia's sunny land he was inclined to roam.
He robbed the rich and he helped the poor; his foes he did destroy.
But never hurt a good man did the wild colonial boy.   CHORUS:

For two long years this daring youth ran on his wild career,
With a head that knew no danger and a heart that knew no fear.
He robbed outright the wealthy squires and their arms he did destroy;
They, trembling, gave their gold up to the wild colonial boy.   CHORUS:

One morning in the outback, wild Jack Duggan rode along,
While listening to the mocking bird singing a cheerful song.
Out jumped three troopers, fierce and grim: Kelly, Davis and Fitzroy.
They all set out to capture him, the wild colonial boy.   CHORUS:

"Surrender now, Jack Duggan; come, you see there's three to one.
Surrender in the Queen's name, sir, you are a plundering son!"
Jack drew two pistols from his belt and glared upon Fitzroy.
"I'll fight, but not surrender!" cried the wild colonial boy.   CHORUS:

He fired a shot at Kelly, quick, which brought him to the ground;
He fired point blank at Davis, too, who fell dead at the sound.
But a bullet pierced his proud young heart from the pistol of Fitzroy,
And that was how they captured him, the wild colonial boy.   CHORUS:

Brennan on the Moor

Willie Brennan "worked" in the Kilworth Mountains between County Cork and County Tipperary. He was executed in Clonmel, County Tipperary, in the early-19th century. Cashel is also in County Tipperary, and was the ancient capital city of the kings of Munster, as well as the stronghold of 10th-century Irish hero Brian Boru.

WITH BRAVADO

Traditional
Words adapted by Mallory Geller

It's___ of a brave young high-way-man, this sto-ry I will tell. His name was Wil-lie Bren-nan and in Ire-land he did dwell. 'Twas on the Kil-worth Moun-tains he com-menced his wild ca-reer, And ma-ny a wealth-y no-ble-man be-fore him shook with fear.

CHORUS:

And it's Bren-nan on the Moor, Bren-nan on the Moor, Bold,___ brave and un-daunt-ed was young Bren-nan on the Moor.

It's of a brave young highwayman, this story I will tell.
His name was Willie Brennan and in Ireland he did dwell.
'Twas on the Kilworth Mountains he commenced his wild career,
And many a wealthy nobleman before him shook with fear.

CHORUS: And it's Brennan on the Moor,
                  Brennan on the Moor,
                  Bold, brave and undaunted was young
                  Brennan on the Moor.

One night he robbed a packman by the name of Peddler Bawn
And they travel'd on together 'til the day began to dawn.
The peddler, seeing his money gone, likewise his watch and chain,
He at once encountered Brennan and robb'd him back again.   *CHORUS:*

Now Brennan, seeing the Peddler as good a man as he,
He says, "My worthy hero, will you come along with me?"
The peddler, being stout-hearted, he threw his pack away,
And he proved a loyal comrade until his dying day.   *CHORUS:*

One day upon the highway as Willie, he went down,
He met the Mayor of Cashel, a mile outside the town.
The Mayor, he knew his features, and he said, "Young man," said he,
"Your name is Willie Brennan—you must come along with me."   *CHORUS:*

Now Brennan's wife had gone to town, provisions for to buy,
And when she saw her Willie, she commenced to weep and cry.
He said, "Hand to me that tenpenny." As soon as Willie spoke,
She handed him a blunderbuss from underneath her cloak.   *CHORUS:*
                                                                For young Brennan...

Then with this loaded blunderbuss the truth I will unfold,
He made the Mayor to tremble, and robbed him of his gold.
One hundred pounds was offered for his apprehension there
So he with horse and saddle to the mountains did repair.   *CHORUS:*
                                                                Did young Brennan...

Now Brennan being an outlaw upon the mountains high,
With cavalry and infantry to take him they did try.
He laughed at them with scorn until, at last, 'twas said
By a falsehearted woman he was cruelly betrayed.   *CHORUS:*
                                                               Was young Brennan...

In the town of Tipperary, in a place they call Clonmore,
They with the mounted cavalry did fight and suffer sore.
He lost his foremost finger, which was shot off by a ball,
So Brennan and his comrades were taken, after all.   *CHORUS:*

They were conveyed to Clonmel jail, strong walls did them surround,
With shackles at their hand and foot, in irons they were bound.
When the judge pronounced their guilt, these words with glee did cry:
"For robbing on the King's highway, you're all condemned to die."   *CHORUS:*

When Brennan heard his sentence, he made one last reply:
"I own that I did rob the rich and did the poor supply;
But in all the deeds that I have done, I took no life away.
The Lord have mercy on your soul against the judgment day!"   *CHORUS:*

Whisky in the Jar

Although they seem to have worked in much the same area, unlike Willie Brennan, this robber's elegy has left posterity not his own name but that of his victim-turned-captor. If the fellow does manage to contact his brother in either Cork or in County Kerry's Killarney, his plan is to move his base of operations northeast 100 miles or so into County Kilkenny.

BRISKLY   Traditional

As I was go-ing ov-er the Kil-ma-gen-ny Moun-tain, I met with Cap-tain Far-rell and his mon-ey he was count-ing. I first pro-duced my pis-tol, and then I drew my ra-pier, Say-ing, "Stand and de-li-ver for I am a bold de-cei-ver."

CHORUS: Wish-a rig-um, dur-um, dah; whack fol the dad-dy o, Whack fol the dad-dy o, there's whis-ky in the jar.

As I was going over the Kilmagenny Mountain,
I met with Captain Farrell and his money he was counting.
I first produced my pistol, and then I drew my rapier,
Saying, "Stand and deliver, for I am a bold deceiver."

CHORUS: Wisha rigum, durum, dah; whack fol the daddy o,
                   Whack fol the daddy o, there's whisky in the jar.

He counted out his money and it made a pretty penny,
I put it in my pocket and I gave it to my Jenny.
She sighed and she swore that she never would deceive me,
But the devil take the women for they never can be easy.   *CHORUS:*

I went into my chamber for to take a slumber;
I dreamt of gold and jewels and sure it was no wonder.
But Jenny took my charges and filled them up with water,
And sent for Captain Farrell to be ready for the slaughter.   *CHORUS:*

'Twas early in the morning before I rose to travel,
The guards were all around me and likewise Captain Farrell.
I then produced my pistol for she stole away my rapier,
But I couldn't shoot the water, so a prisoner I was taken.   *CHORUS:*

If anyone can aid me, it's my brother in the army,
I think that he is stationed in Cork or in Killarney;
And if he'd come and join me we'd go rovin' in Kilkenny.
I swear he'd treat me better than my darling, sporting Jenny.   *CHORUS:*

Saint Patrick Was a Gentleman

From its sound and feel, this song must surely have been born in a music hall. It seems odd to hear a bona fide saint sung about as though he was just one of the boys. Contrary to any attempts to make Saint Patrick a true-born Irishman, this 4th-century cleric was actually of British birth and first came to the Emerald Isle as a slave. Only much later did he return to Christianize the Island—to cast out all its vermin.

WITH FAITH
AND BEGORRAH

Words by Henry Bennet and Mr. Toleken
Music is Traditional

Saint Patrick was a gentleman, he came from decent people;
In Dublin Town he built a church, and on it put a steeple.
His father was a Callaghan, his mother was a Brady,
His aunt was an O'Shaughnessy and his uncle was a Grady.

CHORUS: Then success to bold Saint Patrick's fist
     He was a saint so clever,
     He gave the snakes an awful twist
     And banished them forever.

There's not a mile in Ireland's isle where the dirty vermin musters;
Where'er he put his dear forefoot he murder'd them in clusters.
The toads went hop, the frogs went plop, slap dash into the water,
And the beasts committed suicide to save themselves from slaughter. *CHORUS:*

Nine hundred thousand vipers blue he charm'd with sweet discourses,
And dined on them at Killaloe in soups and second courses.
When blind worms crawling in the grass disgusted all the nation,
He gave them a rise and open'd their eyes to a sense of their situation. *CHORUS:*

The Wicklow hills are very high, and so's the hill of Howth, sir;
But there's a hill much higher still, aye, higher than them both, sir.
'Twas on the top of this high hill Saint Patrick preached the sarmint,
That drove the frogs into the bogs, and bothered all the varmint. *CHORUS:*

The Sash
Me Father Wore

In July, 1690, the signal colour of the victorious Protestants under King William was orange, and the Protestants of Northern Ireland have been known as Orangemen ever since. Every July they put on their orange sashes, pound their huge bass drums and march in commemoration of their ancestors' victory.

An Orangemen song
Traditional

PROUDLY

Sure,— I'm an Ul-ster Or-ange Man, from— Er-in's Is-le I came.— To

see me Glas-gow breth-r-en all of hon-our and of fame,— And to

tell them of me fore-fa-thers who fought in days— of yore;— All

on the twelfth day of Ju-ly, in the sash me fa-ther wore.—

CHORUS:

It's— ould, but it's— beau-ti-ful, it's the best you've ev-er seen,— Been

worn for more than nine-ty years in that lit-tle Isle of Green.— From me

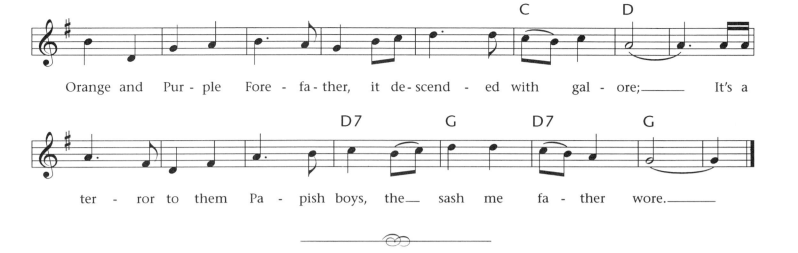

Orange and Pur - ple Fore - fa - ther, it de - scend - ed with gal - ore;_____ It's a

ter - ror to them Pa - pish boys, the__ sash me fa - ther wore._____

Sure, I'm an Ulster Orange Man, from Erin's Isle I came
To see me Glasgow brethren all of honour and of fame,
And to tell them of me forefathers who fought in days of yore;
All on the twelfth day of July, in the sash me father wore.

CHORUS: It's ould, but it's beautiful, it's the best you've ever seen,
            Been worn for more than ninety years in that little Isle of Green.
            From me Orange and Purple Forefather, it descended with galore;
            It's a terror to them Papish boys, the sash me father wore.

So, here I am in Glasgow town, youse boys and girls to see,
And I hope that in good Orange style, you will welcome me.
A true blue blade that's just arrived from that dear Ulster shore;
All on the twelfth day of July, in the sash me father wore.   *CHORUS:*

And when I'm going to leave yeeze all, "Good luck" to youse I'll say,
And as I cross the raging sea, me Orange flute I'll play.
Returning to my native town, to ould Belfast once more,
To be welcomed back by Orangemen, in the sash me father wore.   *CHORUS:*

The Ould Orange Flute

This song manages to take a good-natured stance toward Ireland's "troubles," the centuries-old conflict between Irish Protestants, the Orange, and Irish Catholics, the Green. "Croppies" were rebels in the uprising of 1798.

WITH EXPRESSION

Words by Nugent Bohem

In the Coun - ty Ty - rone, near the town of Dun - gan - non, Where was

ma - ny a ruc - tion me - self had a hand in, Bob Wil - liam - son lived, a

weav - er by trade, And___ all of us thought him a stout Or - ange blade. On the

twelfth of Ju - ly, as it year - ly did come,___ Bob played on his flute to the

sound of the drum. You may talk of your harp, your pi - an - o or lute, But___

none can com - pare with the ould Or - ange flute.

In the County Tyrone, near the town of Dungannon,
Where was many a ruction meself had a hand in,
Bob Williamson lived, a weaver by trade,
And all of us thought him a stout Orange blade.
On the twelfth of July, as it yearly did come,
Bob played on his flute to the sound of the drum.
You may talk of your harp, your piano or lute,
But none can compare with the ould Orange flute.

Now this treacherous scoundrel, he took us all in,
For he married a Papish called Bridget McGinn,
Turned Papish himself and forsook the old Cause,
That gave us our freedom, religion and laws.
Well, the boys of the town made some noise upon it,
And Bob had to fly to the Province of Connaught.
He flew with his wife and fixings to boot,
And along with the others his ould Orange flute.

At chapel on Sundays, to atone for past deeds,
He said Paters and Aves, and counted his beads,
'Til after some time, at the priest's own desire,
He went with that ould flute to play in the choir.
He went with that ould flute to play in the loft,
But the instrument shivered and sighed and then coughed.
When he blew it and fingered it, it made a strange noise,
For the flute would play only, *The Protestant Boys*.

Bob jumped up and started and got in a flutter,
And he put the ould flute in the blessed holy water.
He thought that it might now make some other sound;
When he blew it again, it played, *Croppies, Lie Down!*
And all he did whistle, and finger, and blow,
To play Papish music he found it no go.
Kick the Pope, *The Boyne Water*, and such like 'twould sound,
But one Papish squeak in it could not be found.

At a council of priests that was held the next day
They decided to banish the ould flute away;
As they couldn't knock heresy out of its head,
They bought Bob another to play in its stead.
So, the ould flute was doomed and its fate was pathetic;
It was fastened and burned at the stake as heretic.
As the flames roared around it they heard a strange noise:
'Twas the ould flute still whistling *The Protestant Boys*.

Arthur McBride

This rollicking anti-recruitment song was first collected around 1840, and probably comes from the Donegal area.

SMARTLY   *Traditional*

I had a first cous - in called Ar - thur Mc - Bride, He and I took a

stroll down____ by the sea - side, A - seek - ing good for - tune and

what might be - tide, 'Twas just as the day was a - dawn - ing. Then

af - ter rest - ing we both took a tramp And we met Ser - geant Har - per and

Cor - po - ral____ Cramp, And be - sides a wee drum - mer who beat up for

camp, With his row - dy - dow - dow in the morn - ing.

I had a first cousin called Arthur McBride,
He and I took a stroll down by the seaside,
A-seeking good fortune and what might betide,
'Twas just as the day was a-dawning.
Then after resting we both took a tramp
And we met Sergeant Harper and Corporal Cramp,
And besides a wee drummer who beat up for camp,
With his rowdy-dow-dow in the morning.

He said, "My young fellows, if you will enlist,
A guinea you quickly shall have in your fist,
And besides a crown for to kick up the dust,
And drink the King's health in the morning."
Had we been two such fools as to take the advance,
With the wee bit of money we'd have to run chance;
"For you'd think it no scruple to send us to France,
Where we would be killed in the morning."

He says, "My young fellows, if I hear but one word,
I instantly now will out with my sword,
And into your bodies as strength will afford.
So now, my gay devils, take warning!"
But Arthur and I, we took in the odds,
And we gave them no chance for to launch out their swords;
Our whacking shillelaghs came over their heads,
And paid them right smart in the morning.

As for the young drummer, we rifled his pouch,
And we made a football of his rowdy-dow-dow,
And into the ocean to rock and to roll
And barring the day its returning.
As for the rapier that hung by his side,
We flung it as far as we could in the tide;
"To the devil I bid you," says Arthur McBride,
"To temper your steel in the morning."

The Merry Ploughboy

(Off To Dublin in the Green)

Though this militant song, with its message of beating plowshares into swords, dates from the 1916 Easter Rebellion, its catchy tune is popular even among the politically uninvolved.

REBELLIOUSLY

Traditional

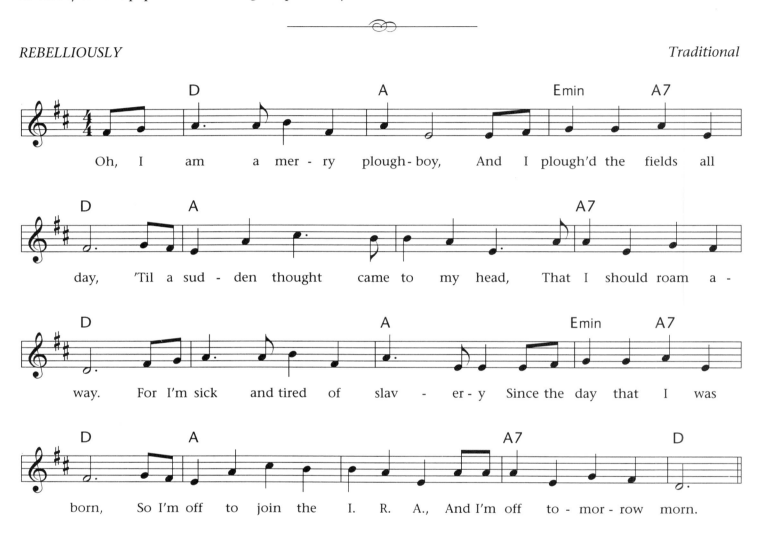

Oh, I am a mer - ry plough - boy, And I plough'd the fields all day, 'Til a sud - den thought came to my head, That I should roam a - way. For I'm sick and tired of slav - er - y Since the day that I was born, So I'm off to join the I. R. A., And I'm off to - mor - row morn.

CHORUS:

And we're all off to Dub - lin in the green, in the green, Where the

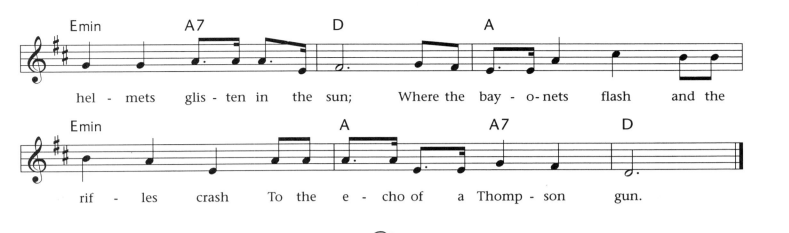

hel - mets glis - ten in the sun; Where the bay - o- nets flash and the

rif - les crash To the e - cho of a Thomp - son gun.

Oh, I am a merry ploughboy,
And I plough'd the fields all day,
'Til a sudden thought came to my head,
That I should roam away.
For I'm sick and tired of slavery
Since the day that I was born,
So I'm off to join the I.R.A.,
And I'm off tomorrow morn.

CHORUS: And we're all off to Dublin in the green, in the green,
Where the helmets glisten in the sun;
Where the bayonets flash and the rifles crash
To the echo of a Thompson gun.

I'll leave aside my pick and spade,
And I'll leave aside my plow,
And I'll leave aside my horse and yoke
For no more I'll need them now.
And I'll leave aside my Mary,
She's the girl who I adore,
And I wonder if she'll think of me
When she hears the cannons roar. *CHORUS:*

And when the war is over,
And dear old Ireland is free,
I'll take Mary to the church to wed
And a rebel's wife she will be.
Some men fight for riches,
Fame and glory is their goal,
But the I.R.A. is fighting for
The land the Saxons stole. *CHORUS:*

The Wearing of the Green

In the mid-19th century, Dion Boucicault took the original version of this tune, which referred to the rebellion of 1798, and wrote the more familiar lyrics we know today. The growing or wearing of shamrocks (from the Irish seamróg, a three-leafed clover), the floral emblem of the Irish, was never actually forbidden, and is here used as a symbol for the expression of Irish nationalism. James Napper Tandy (1740-1803) was a leading figure active in the events surrounding the 1798 rebellion. A "caubeen" is a man's cap or hat.

FERVENTLY

Words by Dion Boucicault
Music is Traditional

O,— Pad-dy dear, and did you hear the news that's go-ing 'round? The Sham-rock is by law for-bid to grow on Ir-ish ground! No— more St. Pat-rick's Day we'll keep, his col-our can't be seen, For there's a blood-y law a-gin' the wear-ing of the green. I— met with Nap-per Tan-dy, and he took me by the hand, And he said, "How's poor old Ire-land, and what way does she stand?" She's the

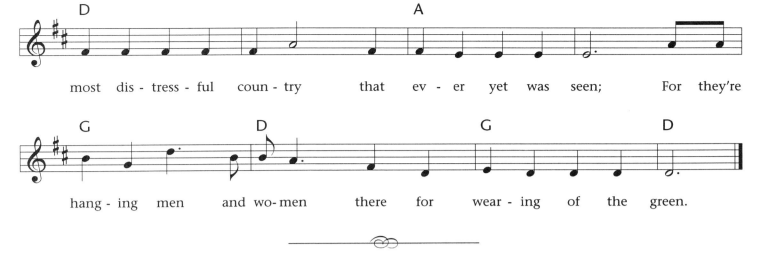

most dis-tress-ful coun-try that ev-er yet was seen; For they're

hang-ing men and wo-men there for wear-ing of the green.

O, Paddy dear, and did you hear the news that's going 'round?
The shamrock is by law forbid to grow on Irish ground!
No more St. Patrick's Day we'll keep, his colour can't be seen,
For there's a bloody law agin' the wearing of the green.
I met with Napper Tandy, and he took me by the hand,
And he said, "How's poor old Ireland, and what way does she stand?"
She's the most distressful country that ever yet was seen;
For they're hanging men and women there for wearing of the green.

Then if the colour we must wear is England's cruel red,
Sure, Ireland's sons will ne'er forget the blood that they have shed.
You may take the Shamrock from your hat and cast it on the sod,
But 'twill take root there and flourish still, though underfoot 'tis trod.
When the law can stop the blades of grass from growing as they grow,
And when the leaves in summertime their verdure dare not show,
Then I will change the colour that I wear in my caubeen,
But 'til that day, please God, I'll stick to the wearing of the green.

But if, at last, our colour should be torn from Ireland's heart,
Her sons with shame and sorrow from the dear old soil will part.
I've heard whisper of a country that lies far beyond the sea,
Where rich and poor stand equal in the light of freedom's day.
O, Erin, must we leave you, driven by the tyrant's hand?
Must we ask a mother's blessing from a strange but happier land?
Where the cruel cross of England's thralldom never shall be seen,
And where, praise God, we'll live and die still wearing of the green.

The Rising of the Moon

Perhaps the moral of this song is to speak softly but carry a sharp pike. John Keegan Casey (1846-1870) was a Fenian from Mullingar who died in prison. He wrote these words about the rebellion of 1798. "Banshee" is taken directly from the Irish badhbh chaointe, meaning a female spirit whose wail is said to warn of approaching death. A "buachaill" (pronounced buck-hul) is an affectionate Irish term for a boy or young man. A "pike" is a weapon consisting of a long wooden pole with a sharp steel blade at the head, used by foot soldiers.

ZEALOUSLY

Words by John Keegan Casey
Air is a slight variant of Wearing of the Green

"O, then, tell me, Sean O' Far-rell, tell me why you hur-ry so?" "Hush me buach-aill, hush and lis-ten," and his cheeks were all a - glow. "I bear or - ders from the Cap-tain, get you rea - dy quick and soon, For the pikes must be to - geth - er by the ris - ing of the moon."

CHORUS:

By the ris - ing of the moon,— by the ris - ing of the moon. For the pikes must be to - geth - er by the ris - ing of the moon.

"O, then, tell me, Sean O'Farrell, tell me why you hurry so?"
"Hush me *buachaill*, hush and listen," and his cheeks were all aglow.
"I bear orders from the Captain, get you ready quick and soon,
For the pikes must be together by the rising of the moon."

CHORUS: By the rising of the moon, by the rising of the moon.
                For the pikes must be together by the rising of the moon.

"O, then, tell me, Sean O'Farrell, where the gath'ring is to be?"
"In the old spot by the river, right well known to you and me.
One word more, for signal token whistle up the marching tune,
With your pike upon your shoulder by the rising of the moon."

CHORUS: By the rising of the moon, by the rising of the moon.
                With your pike upon your shoulder by the rising of the moon.

Out from many a mud-wall cabin, eyes were watching through that night,
Many a manly heart was throbbing for the coming morning light.
Murmurs ran along the valleys, like the banshee's lonely croon,
And a thousand blades were flashing by the rising of the moon.

CHORUS: By the rising of the moon, by the rising of the moon.
                And a thousand blades were flashing by the rising of the moon.

There, beside the singing river, that dark mass of men was seen;
Far above their shining weapons hung their own beloved green.
"Death to every foe and traitor! Forward! Strike the marching tune!
And hurrah, me boys for freedom; 'tis the rising of the moon!"

CHORUS: 'Tis the rising of the moon, 'tis the rising of the moon.
                And hurrah, me boys for freedom; 'tis the rising of the moon!

Well they fought for poor old Ireland, and full bitter was their fate;
O, what glorious pride and sorrow fills the name of Ninety-Eight!
Yet, thank God e'en still are beating hearts in manhood's burning noon,
Who would follow in their footsteps at the rising of the moon!

CHORUS: At the rising of the moon, at the rising of the moon.
                Who would follow in their footsteps at the rising of the moon!

A Nation Once Again

Thomas Davis (1814-1845) of Dublin, one of the founders of the Young Ireland Movement, wrote this powerful rallying song circa 1842. A "fane" is used here to mean a church. The third verse is often omitted from performance because its inclusion justifies rebellion as a religious prerogative.

WITH PASSION

by Thomas Davis

When boy-hood's fire was in my blood I read of an-cient free men, For Greece and Rome who brave-ly stood Three hun-dred men and three men. And then I prayed I yet might see Our fet-ters rent in twain, And Ire-land long a prov-ince be A Na-tion once a-gain!

CHORUS:

A Na-tion once a-gain, A Na-tion once a-gain, And Ire-land long a prov-ince be A Na-tion once a-gain!

When boyhood's fire was in my blood
I read of ancient free men,
For Greece and Rome who bravely stood
Three hundred men and three men.
And then I prayed I yet might see
Our fetters rent in twain,
And Ireland long a province be
A Nation once again!

CHORUS: A Nation once again,
                 A Nation once again,
                 And Ireland long a province be
                 A Nation once again!

And from that time through wildest woe
That hope has shone a far light,
Nor could love's brightest summer glow
Outshine that solemn starlight.
It seemed to watch above my head
In forum, field and fane,
Its angel voice sang 'round my bed:
"A Nation once again!"   *CHORUS:*

It whisper'd, too, that freedom's ark,
And service high and holy,
Would be profaned by feelings dark
And passions vain or lowly;
For freedom comes from God's right hand
And needs a godly train,
And righteous men must make our land
A Nation once again!   *CHORUS:*

So, as I grew from boy to man,
I bent me to that bidding.
My spirit of each selfish plan
And cruel passion ridding.
For thus I hoped some day to aid;
Oh, can such hope be vain?
When my dear country shall be made
A Nation once again!   *CHORUS:*

Saint Patrick's Day

As an instrumental, Saint Patrick's Day is often played quickly and the tune conveys a jaunty, jolly feeling. But when the melody is slowed down enough to allow the singer to perform M.J. Barry's powerful poetry and patriotic vision, the fusion of music and lyrics is truly stirring. "Innisfail" is an old name for Ireland, meaning land of destiny.

ROUSINGLY

Words by M.J. Barry

Oh! blest be the days when the Green Ban-ner float-ed Sub-

lime o'er the moun-tains of free Inn-is-fail; Her sons, to her glo-ry and

free-dom de-vot-ed, De-fi'd the in-vad-er to tread her soil. When

back o'er the main they chas'd the Dane, And gave to re-li-gion and

learn-ing their spoil; When val-or and mind to-geth-er com-bin'd But—

where-fore la-ment o'er the glo-ries de-part-ed? Her

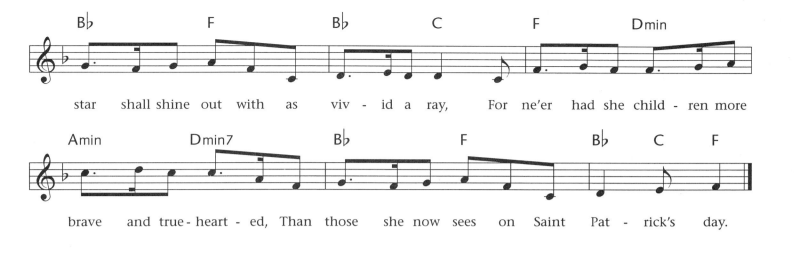

star shall shine out with as viv - id a ray, For ne'er had she child - ren more

brave and true - heart - ed, Than those she now sees on Saint Pat - rick's day.

Oh! blest be the days when the Green Banner floated
Sublime o'er the mountains of free Innisfail;
Her sons, to her glory and freedom devoted,
Defi'd the invader to tread her soil.
When back o'er the main they chas'd the Dane,
And gave to religion and learning their spoil;
When valor and mind together combin'd—
But wherefore lament o'er the glories departed?
Her star shall shine out with as vivid a ray,
For ne'er had she children more brave and true-hearted,
Than those she now sees on Saint Patrick's day.

Her sceptre, alas! pass'd away to the stranger,
And treason surrender'd what valor had held;
But true hearts remain'd amid darkness and danger
Which, 'spite of her tyrants, would not be quell'd.
Oft', oft', thro' the night flash'd gleams of light,
Which almost the darkness of bondage dispell'd;
But a star now is near, her heaven to cheer,
Not like the wild gleams which so fitfully darted,
But long to shine down with a hallowing ray
On daughters as fair, and sons as true-hearted,
As Erin beholds on Saint Patrick's day.

Oh! blest be the hour when, begirt by her cannon,
And hail'd as it rose by a nation's applause,
That flag wav'd aloft o'er the spire of Dungannon,
Asserting for Irishmen Irish laws.
Once more shall it wave o'er hearts as brave,
Despite of the dastards who mock at her cause;
And like brothers agreed, whatever their creed,
Her children inspir'd by those glories departed,
No longer in darkness desponding will stay,
But join in her cause like the brave and true-hearted,
Who rise for their rights on Saint Patrick's day.

Master McGrath

An R-rated dog tail of the Battle of Waterloo... Cup, as told by an Irish wag. It is sometimes said that Master McGrath (pronounced McGraw) provided the Irish with the only victories they ever won on British soil, at the dog races of 1868, 1869 and 1871. Lurgan is in County Armagh, and "Albion" is a mythic name for Britain dating from Roman times.

JUBILANTLY

Words adapted by Mallory Geller
Music is Traditional

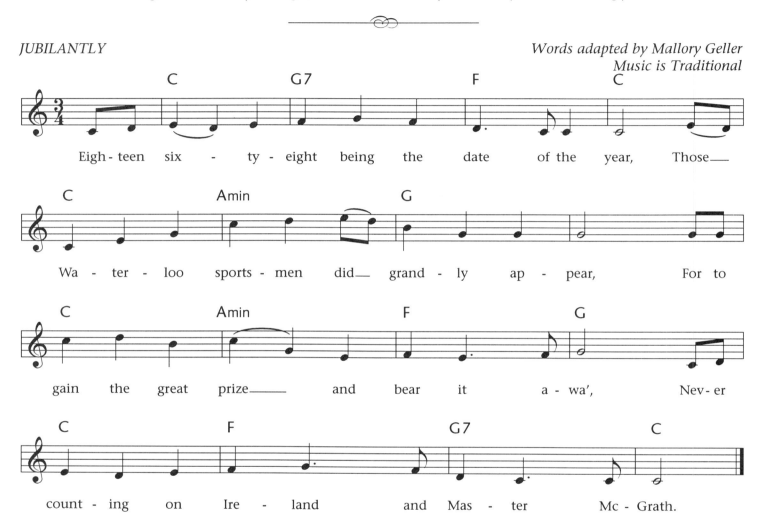

Eigh - teen six - ty - eight being the date of the year, Those— Wa - ter - loo sports - men did— grand - ly ap - pear, For to gain the great prize—— and bear it a - wa', Nev - er count - ing on Ire - land and Mas - ter Mc - Grath.

Eighteen sixty-eight being the date of the year,
Those Waterloo sportsmen, did grandly appear,
For to gain the great prize and bear it awa',
Never counting on Ireland and Master McGrath.

On the twelfth of November, that day of renown,
McGrath and his keeper they left Lurgan town.
John Walsh was the trainer, and soon they got o'er;
On the thirteenth they landed on England's fair shore.

Now, when they arrived there in big London Town,
Those great English sportsmen, they all gathered 'roun',
And one of those gentlemen heav'd a guffaw
Sayin', "Is that the great dog you call Master McGrath?"

A second bold gentlemen standing around
Says: "I don't care a damn for your Irish greyhound."
Still another he sneers, with a scornful "Haw! Haw!
We'll soon humble the pride of your Master McGrath."

Then, Lord Lurgan comes forward and says, "Gentlemen,
If there's any amongst you has money to spend,
For your grand English nobles I don't care a straw—
Here's five thousand-to-one upon Master McGrath."

Oh, McGrath he looks up and he wags his ould tail,
Informing his lordship, "Sure, you're right on the nail.
Don't fear, noble Brownlow, don't fear them agra,
We'll soon tarnish their laurels," says Master McGrath.

Well, White Rose stood uncovered, the great English pride,
Her master and keeper there close by her side;
Then the slips were let loose, and amid a great roar
The greyhounds swept on like great waves to the shore.

As White Rose and the Master they ran head to head,
"I wonder," says Rose, "what took you from your bed?
You should have stayed there in your Irish domain,
And not come to gain laurels on Albion's plain."

"Well, I know," says the Master, "we have wild heather bogs
But, bedad, in old Ireland there's good men and dogs.
Lead on, bold Britannia, give none of your jaw;
Stuff that up your nostrils," says Master McGrath.

Well, the hare she led on just as swift as the wind.
He was sometimes before her and sometimes behind,
Then he jumps on her back and holds up his ould paw,
"Long live the Republic," says Master McGrath.

We've seen many greyhounds that filled us with pride,
In the days that are gone, but it can't be denied,
That the greatest and gamest the world ever saw
Was our champion of champions, ould Master McGrath.

DISCARD

of Titles

Some songs are known by more than one title.
The primary title used in this book is in italics.

⚭